Ava's Curse
STAR CROSSED
NOVEL

WRITTEN BY
BELLE RONDEAU

AVA'S CURSE
Star Crossed Novel

In no way is it legal to reproduce, duplicate, or transmit any part of this document in either electronic means or in printed format. Recording of this publication is not allowed unless with written permission from the publisher. All Rights Reserved.

This book is a work of fiction, and all characters, places, events, and names are the product of the Author's imagination. Any resemblance to other events, locations, or persons, living or deceased is purely coincidental. The Author reserves all rights to be recognized as the owner of this work.

The information provided herein is stated to be truthful and consistent, on that any liability in terms of inattention or otherwise, by any usage or abuse of any policies, processes, or directions contained within is the solitary and utter responsibility of the recipient reader. Under no circumstances will any legal responsibility or blame be held against the publisher for any reparation damages, or monetary loss due to the information herein, either directly or indirectly.

Respective Authors own all copyrights not held by the publisher. The information herein is offered for informational purposes solely and is universal as so.

Copyright © 2023 Isobel Rondeau

In birth we grow

In life we learn

In death we remember

You did great

See you soon

4 hearts forever

In loving memory

J,T,D & M

WORD TRANSLATION

Clos	Rest
Haggis	savory pudding made from sheep's pluck, onion, oatmeal, suet, spices, salt, stock cooked in an animal stomach though artificial casing is commonly used now
Helo	Hello
Jostaberries	purple berries found on thornless bushes
Mucham	Extinguish!
Neeps	Turnips
Seanmhair	Grandmother
Tattie tikki	Potatoes boiled, mashed, flattened, add neeps, and fold in. fried in oil
Wicche	Witch, wizard, or sorcerer

Coineachan is a term of endearment applied to a child.

CONTENTS

WORD TRANSLATION iv

1. Katherine Macsymon 1
2. Ava Ten Years Later 3
3. Enid 31
4. Professor Craig 37
5. Ava 47
6. Freedom 55
7. Ava 59
8. Enid 81
9. Ava 89
10. Freedom 95
11. Enid 101
12. Ava 107
13. Ian 117
14. Rose 127
15. Professor Craig 131
16. Enid 137
17. Majestic 139
18. Freedom 151

19.	Enid	157
20.	Ava	161
21.	Professor Craig	167
22.	Tyler	175
EPILOGUE		177

CHAPTER ONE
Katherine Macsymon

I gasped on my last breath as freezing cold water filled my lungs to bursting. I struggled and kicked. Trying my hardest to fight the inevitable. I felt my arms get heavy, my body losing the urge to fight any longer. I could see my daughter, Ava, her beautiful laughing blue eyes, her coral, pink-tinged lips. I could almost feel her soft little arms wrap me in a hug goodbye, one last time. I almost had it, the cure, I had it. I was on the right track. Now, I would die, like all my ancestors. At fifty years old my time had come to leave this earth. Oh, how I wished I could take it back. Every minute I had been angry at Ava, and her best friend, Enid. They would need each other now. I had taught them both, everything I had learned. I would miss my best friend, Lisa, she had to be strong and protect them all now. The gypsy was coming, he would be here soon. I closed my eyes and saw my mother, her golden hair long and flowing, it looked like sun-spun straw, and her sparkling blue eyes were calm and steady. She gestured for me to come forward. Behind her I could see my grandmother, my great-grandmother, and many others, their eyes all locked on me. They were waiting for me to join them. I hadn't seen my mom for so long, I missed her. Wait a minute, the curse, I need to help my little Ava, but my mind goes quiet. I willingly drift toward my mother. I welcome her warm embrace while my lifeless body floats in the cold water of the lake.

The curse has claimed another.

In another part of the world, we watched from afar, how long would this continue. We would most likely have to intervene before the worst could happen. We need to set some things in motion. Our son Ian would be the best we could send to help the humans.

CHAPTER TWO
Ava Ten Years Later

How had I gotten here? I am a normal twenty-year-old female. Everything about me screams normal, long blond hair, blue eyes, average five-foot-six-inch height. My name is Ava MacSymon a third-year student at the University of Edinburgh. The only different quality I had from everyone else was that I was a witch. That last bit I had learned from my now-dead mother, Katherine, who was also a witch. As were my grandmother and my great-grandmother and so on and so on.

My current situation was all my fault, how could I let one little disagreement turn into this personal storm of emotion? My best friend, Enid, laughed at me when I told her I wanted to study Celtic at University.

Her exact words were, "What can a Degree in Celtic get you nowadays? It is not a viable way to pay bills." She went on to say I should just join her in Business classes, no thank you. I had been doing so well, taking extra classes during breaks, doing extra assignments for higher marks, and making university my whole life. No parties, no TV marathons with friends, and definitely no boys. I had one final semester and still no answer to the questions I have asked myself since I was ten years old. Why me? How did I fit into all this magic? What did I need to do to figure it all out and where did I start?

First things first, I needed to go talk to Enid. I couldn't let her believe I meant all the mean words I had said. She's my best friend and has been since we were born, our moms were best friends and when my mom suddenly died at age fifty, Enid's family took me in and raised me like their own child. I had never told anyone I was a witch, but I thought Enid must know. Over the years I wanted to tell her and her parents, but the feelings always passed. Now, here I am, stuck with no guidance only my wit and keen sense of intuition to help figure out this curse on me. Well, I think it's a curse, I kept having uneasy dreams of drowning, like my mom. My intuition tingled whenever I left the house alone. My mind knew it was in trouble, but my body didn't agree.

The warm rays of the June sunshine, a nice change from the rain, kept me walking instead of taking the train. At this time of day, I knew I would find Enid at the library studying business journals or something like that. As I got closer to the main library the clouds started to roll in, so much for my sunny walk. Immediately entering the double doors into the main library, I took a right down the cold, stone hallway to the class libraries. As I entered the department, I looked to my right but didn't see Enid in her usual spot. The bright fluorescent lights beside the hydroponic growing tower drew my eyes, she loved sitting beside the greenery. She said she could hear it growing ... like she could do that. I did a loop around the study area, but no Enid. Before I could wonder where else she could likely be, a nerdy business type, complete with black-rimmed glasses and a tousled mess of dark hair, approached me.

"Are you looking for Enid?" he quietly asked.

Quickly giving him the once over, noticing his piercing brown eyes, I answered with my own question, "Have you seen her in the last hour?"

My eyes glanced around the area once more before he answered in a quiet, deep voice "She was here and was sad or maybe mad, I think she had trouble concentrating and she left here after about ten minutes. I was going to follow her to see if she was ok, but I have this paper due tomorrow so…" his voice faded awkwardly away when I didn't comment. I hurriedly choked out a thanks before I bolted to the main lobby. I noticed his quizzical look before I turned. So, embarrassing. How could I stay in a conversation when my eyes got blurry, and ringing burned in my ears? Wishing the nauseous feeling would go away I stopped and leaned against the cold stone wall of the linguistics library. *Tyler*, my mind gave me a name. Then quick as that it was gone. In my panic, I failed to notice my feet leading the way to the place I spent so much time during regular class sessions. I slowly regained my sensibilities, looked around, and there, tucked into a reading nook with a comfy pillow surrounding her was Enid. I breathed a sigh of relief and started towards her. Noticing that her dark, curly chestnut-colored hair was up in a messy bun, her feet tucked underneath her, and glasses perched on her tiny nose. I knew this was her standard studying pose. Whatever she was reading in the linguistic library had her full attention.

"Hey." I quietly said as I nudged her shoulder.

Enid gasped loudly and snapped shut the book she was reading. Before she could put the book under her butt, I grabbed it and almost shouted, but, remembered where I was.

Angrily I bit my lip and growled, "What are you reading up on Celtic history and witchcraft for?"

My thoughts swirled around like a hurricane, trying to grasp at any logical straw, I took a deep breath and said, "If you had any questions, I could have answered them, I know these books and maps almost as well as the authors." I paused and looked into her deep brown eyes which brimmed with tears, and I said, "I'm sorry about everything Enid, please let me answer your questions."

With a soft gasp, one lone tear escaped Enid's eye and rolled down her porcelain skin. I sat down on a cushion beside her and held the book out towards her. With a sigh, I watched as Enid took a breath and sat up straight, she placed her hands together in her lap and looked at me.

She had absently pushed her glasses up and with a gentle smile she said to me, "I know exactly who and what you are, I have known my whole life. You're a witch."

I gulped, breathless, and asked how she knew. In her own words, Enid explained what she knew. Our mothers were best friends as well as our grandmothers and great-grandmothers and so on. She explained that she was more than my best friend. What could be more important than that? Enid said we were a part of a destiny, a destiny that we had to travel together. To my surprise, she compared herself to a witch familiar, most commonly an animal. She and her family were bound to ours and always would be. She said her family had been charmed into being protectors for my family, to the female born every forty years. Being a protector basically meant that she guided me to do stuff and stay out of any bad situations. She quickly drew my attention to the family tree that my mother had left in my baby book, making the connection between that and her family. Too stunned to say anything I tried to listen to her words and make my own connections. In her version of the story, which I knew by heart, my mother had spoken of this every night, her female ancestors took an oath by a wicche in the fifteenth century, to look out for our lineage and ensure that we made it to the year 2030 AD. That Enid knew that much about me and my family, certainly bewildered me, why hadn't she ever hinted that she knew? All the sleepovers, the secrets from the time we were five, the teen girls who had teased her and had called her a nerd, the sneaking out of windows to go to parties we were not allowed to attend. Enid had never asked for my supernatural help. As we marathon-watched wizard and witch movies, she never let on she knew or even believed. I realized that she wasn't getting emotional because of our earlier argument but because she was finally able to open her heart and let all her feelings out for the first time in our twenty-year friendship. I grabbed her and gave her the hardest hug I could and let her know that I was happy we had no more secrets between us.

To which she hastily replied, "Well, I have one more."

I laughed and said, "Well it couldn't be bigger than this one."

Enid went on to tell me about her boyfriend, yup first time I had heard about him. It seemed that during her first year at university, the Business Communications class had set up online profiles, so they could all communicate more efficiently when doing group assignments. Her group thought it would be fun to set up an online dating profile and she had accidentally met, Ian, her boyfriend of two years. I had no idea he existed. I noticed how she smiled when she spoke of him, I knew he must be important so I asked when I could meet this mystery guy. Enid said it was about time he met her whole family and would set something up right away. The library was getting dark and a glance at my watch told me dinner time had come and gone. We were so busy talking we never noticed how the hours had rushed by. Enid and I gathered her stuff up and I told her to leave the books behind she wouldn't need them with me around.

We walked arm in arm and skipped over the puddles from the rainstorm that had silently stormed while we were inside the library. We were talking so fast that we overlapped each other's stories and inserted our own views. We both failed to notice the shadows which followed us. We failed to hear the snap of a camera that captured pictures of our smiling faces and we barely had time to see the ball of fire that exploded before our very eyes. Enid gasped and tried to block me from its heat, but I was faster, I shot my hand out and exclaimed "mucham!" The fireball disappeared in a puff of orange smoke.

"Ava, we better get home." Enid's voice trembled as we watched the smoke disintegrate before us.

Wearily, we made our way to the train station and headed home. Our good mood was silenced while we watched for shadows and movement in the bushes not knowing who or what we were looking for. We walked from Haymarket station to the grounds of Wester Coates Garden uninterrupted. Seeing the big house with its welcoming lights along the walking path made the knot in my stomach ease and breathing became easier the closer we got. Although I hadn't lived in this house with my mom, I had spent many days and nights with Enid and her family, and for the last ten years, this had been my home. We climbed the stone stairs and opened the heavy wooden door; we took off our shoes and both breathed a sigh of relief as we stepped into the reception hall appreciating the warmth of the dark wood-paneled walls and sunk our bare feet into the plush white carpet. The lights of the centuries-old chandelier danced off the mirrors scattered around the room. Lisa, Enid's mom, came running into the room and stopped short when she could see we were both unharmed.

"Are you both ok?" Lisa asked.

Quickly Enid replied, "I told Ava, everything we know, and yes we are both fine."

Lisa hugged both of us and ushered us into the kitchen for a late dinner and a warm drink to calm the chills that were setting in. It's funny now that I looked back on all the sideways glances and hushed conversations I had encountered within this house over the years. Never bothering to question, but always wondering what was going on. I also had some pressing questions regarding my mother and grandmother. But those could wait till morning. There was a warm plate of Haggis with neeps and Tattie tikki waiting for us at the large wooden kitchen island where Enid and I had spent countless hours doing homework. We took turns telling Lisa, and her husband Mitch, about our day and that we had squabbled about my choice of major at university. Which now seemed like such a trivial matter. I wondered out loud why someone would throw a fireball at us. I saw the quick glance between Lisa and Mitch, they stood and started cleaning the dinner mess Enid and I had made.

"Why don't you girls get ready for bed, we could watch a bit of telly before turning in." Lisa instructed.

Feeling exhaustion starting to creep in I made my way to my bedroom where the fluffy bed beckoned to me. I opened my closet and ran my hand lovingly over all the fabric, every piece had been hand-picked by me and paid for out of a generous allowance allotted to me on my mother's passing. I loved shopping. The colour, texture, and array of different fabrics. I loved the atmosphere and the anticipation of finding the perfect fit to add to my wardrobe. I opened my dresser and took out my comfy family movie night pajamas. I slipped on my robe and slippers and padded to the washroom, cleansed my face, and removed my rose gold watch, a gift from Lisa and Mitch on my eighteenth birthday. I noticed little freckles had appeared on my clean skin, darn that sun. Only a couple of hours and already freckles had appeared, thank goodness I hadn't burned my skin. I vowed as I did every summer, to wear a hat and stay out of the sun. My long blonde hair was loosely tied back in a ponytail, my teeth brushed, and night cream applied I headed down the carpeted stairs to the movie room and my comfortable recliner. Happily, I noticed my popcorn and iced tea were waiting for me. Enid was already there munching her buttery popcorn. They had waited for my arrival to start the movie. I realized sadly that these nights came far less often than when we were younger. Happily, I settled in and as the lights went down, I was comforted that these three people, whom I had known and loved my entire life, were with me right now.

    I awoke with a start; the room was cloaked in darkness. I tapped my phone it was 3:35 in the morning. I didn't even remember watching the end of the movie. I was the only one left in the living room, I put my blanket aside, the cool air made me shiver and I quietly made my way through the darkened hallways to my bedroom. Closing my door, I headed to the bathroom and turned on the salt lamp, the warm pink glow lit the walls, it was one of my favorite gifts from Enid. She said it had healing properties, all I knew was that it made me feel safe and warm. I guess in her eyes making me feel safe and warm was her way of protecting me, but I was unsure of what I needed protecting from. I walked back to my big bed, climbed in, and shivered as the cool flannel sheets, a necessity in Scotland, began to warm. Snug and warm I slowly drifted off to sleep when suddenly I recalled what had woken me up earlier. A hint of a dream came back to me.

Cloudy and out of focus, my mom and I flying a kite at the city park, in the open space a dog barking and running after a bouncing red ball and running back to its owner. Children's echoing laughter and an ice cream truck playing its musical song over a tinny speaker. Me, running towards the truck delighting in the wind on my face, when suddenly my mom's horrified face. She dropped the kite string, I watched as it billowed up higher than ever and floated away in the gusty wind, never to be seen again. She lunged after me and grabbed me right off the ground, turned, and sprinted towards the dense trees. The barking dog continued barking, the children's laughter faded and louder and louder I heard the music of the ice cream truck. My mom stopped and grabbed what looked like a twig from a tree and started to talk to it, the ground shook, my eyes got blurry my head hurt so much, what was going on?

And that's it, that was when I woke up. What kind of message was that? I lay down and went over the dream again, in bits and pieces. I had forgotten some parts. My memory was getting fuzzy. I sensed the daylight trying to make its way into my window, the sun was starting to rise. I glanced at my phone again, 4:39 in the morning, this would be a long day if I didn't get a couple more hours of sleep. I grabbed the duvet, turned over, took a deep breath, and let it out slowly. I cleared my mind, quickly, softly I said "clos" and drifted off for a dreamless sleep.

The next morning, I had a full Scottish breakfast. Yogurt with muesli, fresh-cut fruit, oatcakes, and fresh raspberry jam, followed by a steaming bowl of porridge with currants and brown sugar and a slice of golden toast with orange marmalade. Finished off with half a tomato with cheese melted on top a hard-boiled egg and baked beans. By the time I finished my pot of tea and honey, I was prepared to face the day. I looked at Enid and we both laughed, how have we eaten like this and kept in such great shape? Lisa and Mitch both entered the kitchen to make another pot of tea. My Gaelic Linguistics instructor followed in behind them. I was surprised but gave a little wave and said good morning. Professor Simpson looked grave and a bit uncomfortable. He gave a quick nod of greeting to Enid and came to stand in front of me.

"Helo Ava," he spoke, in his bold straightforward tone. "I heard you had a bit of a fright at the library yesterday, how are you feeling today?"

I swiveled my gaze to Enid and then to Lisa, "How…" I started to ask and quickly realized my favorite teacher, who I learned so much from, was not who I thought he was. I looked back at Professor Simpson and answered slowly, while my brain caught up on what everyone else in the room knew.

"I'm doing fine, as is Enid, thank you for asking." I took Enid's empty plate and put it on mine then walked to the sink and rinsed them. I turned and asked my most pressing question, "Who are you really?"

Professor Simpson smiled sadly and said, "I'm your professor. My name is Craig Simpson. I am also a warlock. I have been in your life and your family's lives for longer than I can remember. I have been on the fringes making sure you received everything you needed."

I tried not to interrupt but the question seemed to just slip out.

"If you're really a warlock, why did my mother still die? Why didn't you stop it? She was in a boating accident and drowned surely you could have stopped that." My voice broke and a sob escaped before I could catch it.

Professor Simpson smiled sadly once again and said, "I am no closer to breaking your lineage curse than I was three hundred years ago. Every fifty years my heart breaks at my futile attempts to keep your female ancestors alive. It seems so senseless; I fear I won't ever be able to figure it out."

I gasped as I heard the reason, not knowing this part, my mom never shared that truth with me. I suppose when you are ten years old you don't want to know you are cursed and will die.

I put the information away to think about later, and asked another question, "Who do you think tried to hurt Enid and I last night? What did they want?"

Settling down into the chair I just vacated, Professor Craig Simpson cleared his throat and took a sip of the tea Lisa had just placed in front of him. I wandered over and sat down beside him. Cheekily I wondered if I should have brought a pen and paper to take notes.

He smirked and said, "A pen and paper would be a good idea."

My mouth agape, I stared at him with new eyes. His hair was a shock of red, his bright eyes showed wisdom and warmth, his glasses were perched on his crooked nose, and a birthmark shaped like a crescent moon graced the left of his mouth. Not a gorgeous man but a handsome one.

"Can you hear all my thoughts?" I asked him.

"Not every thought but I had to be able to hear yours when you were far away just to make sure no trouble came to you or Enid." He glanced at Enid, whose cheeks had turned a light pink. She hadn't known about this type of protection.

I looked toward him again. I needed to hear the whole truth "Are you able to tell the whole story to me or should I start looking for my own answers?"

He looked around at all of us and said, "Let me start at the beginning, we should move into the living room. We would be much more relaxed and comfortable in there." He rose and Enid and I both followed.

Lisa and Mitch both moved at the same time, Lisa grabbed a new pot of tea and honey while Mitch grabbed some freshly baked scones and jelly, they followed the Professor, Enid, and me down the hallway and into the spacious sitting room. The room reminded me of a seanmhair house, white chintz furniture with crochet doilies on the backs, wooden coffee, and end tables with soft light lamps on them. A family portrait, which included me, taken five years ago hung above the mantle. A large stone fireplace with stacked, chopped wood lay on each side of the firebox. The outdoor patio sliding doors were in the middle of large glass windows that overlooked the green gardens below. The sun would be shining brightly if the new windows hadn't been lined with tint. I thought of all the stormy nights I had sat here watching the rain pour down the windows. Counting the beats between thunder to see how far off the storm was. I cried because I missed my mom, Lisa always found me and hugged me and cried with me because she missed her best friend too. Lisa always had a mug of hot chocolate and some cookies to offer, and we would talk for hours about her and my mom, she told me stories of how they got into trouble as teenagers, bucking their mothers and sneaking out of the house.

Craig cleared his throat and took a sip of tea. I stopped my memories from overwhelming me and turned toward him, walked to the couch, and sat on the edge of the seat. Enid sat on the floor by my feet. Lisa sat on the couch by me while Mitch and Professor Craig each took a seat in the matching white wing-backed chairs.

Professor Craig smiled at me and began, "It was 1680, the year was terrible, it was the beginning of what we now call *the killing time*. So many deaths, just governments wanting power, I was barely out of my teens and trying to help the people survive. I had just finished gathering some herbs for medicines needed to help the sick when a beautiful young lady ran straight into my arms, I quickly grabbed the basket holding my precious bundles before the contents could spill out. That was how I met her. Her name was Edina, her hair was the color of straw, her eyes a cornflower blue, and she was by far the most beautiful miss I had ever seen, it took me a brief second to realize she was yelling, crying for help. Behind her, a dark, young gypsy followed. His dark gaze followed her every move. His loose ribboned clothing billowed in the wind, and the gold of his shoe buckles jingled as he strode toward her, toward me. I put her behind me and addressed the gypsy loudly, `Leave her now or I shall report you to the knights of Lord Chancellor, the Duke of Rothes!`

He bellowed that she belonged to him, and he would take her and be gone. Firmly I stayed where I was, I hid the beautiful trembling girl behind me. I inquired how the miss belonged to him as she did not have the flowing, colorful dress of a gypsy and the gypsy man stated that he had won her in a game of chance that her father had lost. The girl was his. I had just enough coin with me not to gamble with her life. I asked how much she would be worth to him, and he smiled widely, half of his teeth were rotted black.

He said, `I need a sheep and two chickens along with a rooster.`

I thought to bargain but felt the slight girl tremble at my back. `I will supply you with these items tomorrow dawn at the town gate, you must leave the girl with me now.`

He agreed and with a flash of colored ribbon, he was gone. I turned to the young miss her face was streaked with tears.

`Thank you sir!` she cried and turned to run.

I hastily grabbed for her arm and said, 'You are not safe yet, please come with me I can get you home.' She sobbed and said her father would not take her back. I looked into her endless blue eyes and promised her I would take care of her. We went to the church where I had a small room and we talked long into the evening.

The next dawn I strode to the town gate with a goat and two chickens along with a mean rooster. I was a few minutes late and I hoped the gypsy had waited for me. I needed him to take the animals from me so I could keep the girl safe. The gypsy was there and glared at me as I approached. I noticed his puffy, red-rimmed eyes, but I ignored those signs as weakness. He took the animals with him and tossed back a swig from the pouch hanging around his neck, then turned and walked away. No words were exchanged, and I watched him for as long as I could to make sure he didn't turn around. I made my way back to the old church, named St Margaret, which was under restoration work, where we had taken refuge. I woke Edina, she was even lovelier than the day before. Her hair was a little mussed from her run and her exhausted tussled sleep. As she rose from the hay where she had lain, a little smell of gunpowder followed her. The old church was used for storage up until about three years earlier. It would be breathtaking once construction to repair the crumbling walls was completed. Her large, blue eyes blinked awake, and a gentle smile graced her lips. We walked the town and visited the milliner and we spoke at length about her family, her sad eyes glittered with tears as she spoke of her mother and sisters. We went back to the church and spoke to the priest who agreed to immediately marry us."

I gasped aloud as I realized he knew my great great great however many grandmothers. Not only knew, but he would be my great great great however many grandfathers. The only one? I had a family member of my own, someone alive.

Professor Craig continued speaking in his gravelly voice, "I knew we had to flee, and I told Edina why. I told her I was a wicche and the animals that the gypsy had taken were not exactly animals. Edina laughed saying that the gypsy had deserved what was coming to him. I was very happy to see the sparkle in her eyes and her mouth curved up into a smile instead of a frown. We loaded our wagon and headed north, happily looking forward to our new home and life. And it was splendid, we had a child, a very bright and beautiful girl, and Edina had ten wonderful years with her. She taught her everything she could until she suddenly died, she drowned while gathering fish for dinner, just days after sweet Emma's tenth birthday. I continued and tried to keep our little Emma happy. She was sad but the animals loved and protected her. She grew and loved and birthed a female child in her fortieth year, she also had ten years with her daughter and then suddenly died, she slipped, hit her head, and fell off the fishing boat we had. It was shortly after her daughter's tenth birthday. At the time of the events, I did not know of the curse. I was in mourning for my dear Edina and our child Emma. Years passed by and as I walked the countryside keeping tabs on the lineage of my beautiful Edina, I noticed a pattern. By this time, I had grown into an old man and so I decided to keep young with an easy spell and observe as only a teacher could."

I almost broke my silence to ask how he liked teaching over the last two hundred years or so, he must be a very patient warlock.

Craig continued with his tale. "Around 1880, I happened upon a group of travelers passing through the town of Edinburgh, I thought I recognized one man with long dark hair and shiny gold buckles on his boots, as the man turned toward me, he smiled, and his black rotted teeth shook me to the core. It was him, the same gypsy who I had sold the animals to in exchange for Edina's life. He strode toward me and inquired how I was and how my children were and if I had cried when my dear wife left me. I stood up straight and asked what he meant by that, and he laughed and said he cursed the women for four hundred years, one hundred years for each animal cheated from him, by me. I crumbled to the ground and sobbed, knowing it was my greed that had cursed the lady I had loved with my whole heart. His parting words chilled me to the bone as at the end of the curse the lineage would stop, knowing my beautiful Edina would be gone I begged how to undo the curse. He laughed and said only one who paid the price before the end could cure the curse, with a bang and a swirl of ribbon the gypsy was gone."

Craig slouched in his chair, put his hands in his hair, and bowed his head. With a deep sigh, he removed his hands and straightened up.

He looked into my eyes and said, "You reminded me so much of her, the first time I saw you at your mother's funeral. You were only ten years old, and I thought you were identical to her with just a bit darker hair. You had the same cornflower blue eyes that sparkled when you laughed, but that day they glittered with tears, just as Edina's had the first time, I met her. I wanted to run and grab you up in a hug and explain everything, but then I noticed Lisa and Mitch and little Enid clutching your hand so tight. After you all left, I noticed one person who had stayed at your mother's grave. Sitting on a black chair meant for family members, I was drawn to him and recognized the tingle when another warlock was close by. His gaze met mine and he stood and introduced himself as Majic, a warlock who had heard the gypsy spew the curse but was unable to stop it. In turn, he found my Edina and made friends with her, when our child, Emma, was born he charmed her with a best friend and protector. A bird, who made sure she would always take the right path and steer clear of any danger. As the years continued the protector changed to take many forms and in the last one hundred fifty years it has been a female best friend. The warlock admitted his time was finally coming to an end on this earth and he was worried the protective spell cast on our lineage would expire when he did. Together we worked madly to find a cure to break the curse but to no avail. Last night the warlock, Majic, took his final breath. I am now the only warlock that I know of, and my time is surely coming to an end soon, as well. The fireball that was thrown at you and Enid was just a warning, I am sure. However, I am not sure how to proceed just yet."

I sat and stared at him. How could this timid man whom I have only known for the last three years be a part of my family?

I looked at Lisa and quietly asked, "How long have you known? How long have you known that my professor was my great-great grandfather? My family? My only biological family?"

She calmly took my hand in hers and said "Craig introduced himself to me at your mother's funeral, I was so devastated, I forgot most of what he said that day except that you were important to him, and my family was to keep you safe. He disappeared after that until you started university three years ago."

I gently removed my hand, my insides were twisted up and turned around, so many secrets, my whole life had been secrets, kept from me, from my friends. Would Enid be my best friend if she hadn't been bewitched to be my protector? As if she heard my silent questions, Enid turned and scooted up beside me on the couch.

She hugged me and whispered into my ear, "I love you for you, not for any spell, you're like my sister and always will be."

I hugged her tight and turned to my professor, my grandfather, how should I address him now?

"You can call me Craig if you'd like." He answered without me asking him out loud.

"Ok," I said, "The first rule of conversation in the twenty-first century, is you have to be asked questions aloud before you can answer. Second, what does the death of Majic, have to do with the fireball tossed at Enid and me last night?"

"Well, according to Majic, the goat, rooster, and two chickens meant to go to the family of the black-haired gypsy man and feed them for the year, disappeared after the moon set two times. The objects I had transformed returned to their original form or maybe they just disappeared. Most of the members of the gypsy`s family died from lack of food and the gypsy man almost died from fever after drinking water from the nearest lake. In his grief, he tried to find Edina and me, but I had cloaked us well enough. Until he found me in my grief once Edina and then Emma had passed on. I think the fireball was meant to warn you, Ava; the gypsy family wants you. I am not sure why though."

I was quiet as I took all the information in. Lisa and Mitch sat with their hands clasped in their laps, heads bowed. I glanced over at Enid; her big brown eyes were still watery while tears streaked down her cheeks.

She gulped, took a steadying breath, and said, "What are we looking at, now that Majic has passed on? I know how I feel, and I know I must protect Ava from the gypsy man. But I'm unsure where he is. I feel safe in this house, but we can't stop living our lives and hide out here forever."

Mitch looked up and replied, "Your mom and I have had wards placed around the house and gardens, no warlock, other than Craig, could enter. We must build them up again now that Majic is gone. The best thing to do would be to act normal, keep on going to school, and let your mom and I handle things around here."

Craig got up from the chair and knelt before me, "I know you must have a million questions Ava; I will answer the best I can, but I really must head to the university. There is a lead on a young warlock in Canada. I faintly sense him. I must continue to look near and far for help. I alone cannot fight the curse on our family."

He rose and looked at Mitch, "I need to be closer to Ava, I do not wish to intrude but might I use your guest house by the stream?"

"Of course," replied Mitch "I will have the house prepared for you by tomorrow."

Craig smiled and said, "I must be heading home now, thank you for your hospitality, I can show myself out." With one last glance at me, Craig left us alone.

I had a lot of questions and as I looked at Lisa, Mitch, and Enid, they were looking back at me waiting for me to say something. I stood and walked to the big windows, looked at the lush green gardens, our little fire pit, and chairs, a little brown bird grabbed a snack from the bird feeder. I could see Edinburgh Castle off in the distance looking down from its high perch just off Princes Street. Everything looked so normal. The same as it had for years. My thoughts rushed around my mind in a jumble, and I knew I needed out. I closed my eyes and pictured my mom and my grandmother, who looked so like her. I turned and smiled at my adoptive family.

"I need to figure out this curse, I'm twenty years old and according to Professor Simpson, that means I have thirty more to figure it out. I don't have a lot of information except a gypsy man cursed my ancestor because he felt cheated. There was a sympathetic warlock named Majic, who helped by giving my family a protector, and now he's gone. I will have to assume that his protection is gone now too."

Enid gasped and said, "No it's not!"

I looked at her, smiled, and said, "You are my very best friend but what if that's all you are? I know you all care a great deal about me, but this is something I think I have to do on my own. I wouldn't be able to stand it if anything were to happen to any of you."

I glanced up into Lisa's eyes, "You were my mom's best friend, you knew her better than anyone else, did she mention any of this to you?"

Lisa looked at me, her kind eyes were sad, and said "No, your mom was a kind and caring soul she had no idea I was her protector. Like I said earlier, I didn't even know about Craig until her funeral."

I quietly asked her, "Do you think she kept secrets from you? Because she told me bedtime stories from the time I can remember, and now, I realize they were not just made-up bedtime stories. They were real stories meant to help me. Guide me when I needed answers. She told me of a tall red-haired man sent to help me and I was to trust him. I am assuming she meant Professor Craig. The bad black-haired man who meant us girl's harm. The gypsy man Craig spoke about. The church where our ancestors were married, she told me all of this."

As I recounted the stories from my childhood, I remembered the Scots Pine treasure box put away in the farthest corner of my closet. A gift from my mother when I was about nine years old: she told me to put my treasures in it and keep it safe. I remember she told me that a stick was her first treasure and I looked in my new box, I saw a stick in it. My mom laughed and said it was important to her, it came from her mom, who got it from her mom. Over the years I had put many little trinkets in the box. An outing with my mom to The Jolly Giant toy store always brought a little toy but I haven't taken the box of treasures out for at least five years.

I looked at my little adoptive family, they had taken care of me for the last ten years. I needed a bit of space and some fresh air.

"I think I need some time to process, I'm going to walk around the gardens, I will be fine," I put my hand up to Enid, who was getting up as if she was going to come with me, "I need some time alone, please understand."

Enid sat back down and said "Of course. I will be in my room if you need to talk when you get back." Enid got up and quickly hugged me then went up the stairs to her room.

Lisa and Mitch stood and began to gather the leftover tea and scones. With a glance at me, before they walked out of the room, Mitch reminded me to take my phone when I left.

I walked to the front door, stopped by the hall closet, and retrieved a light jacket. I slipped out of my slippers and put on my trainers, maybe a little run would help. Out the main door, I turned left to the rough pathway around the stone house, I stopped to appreciate the yellow petals of marigolds scattered throughout the walkway. The sweet smell of the Burnet Roses in full bloom followed me as I strode quickly to the garden hedges. The tall greens engulfed me in their forest-like smell. I loved walking the garden trails, sometimes walking to the end and sitting at the bench watching the Water of Leith go by. I knew I had to figure out a way to break the curse. I headed towards the water; the walk would be a good thirty minutes. While I walked, I went over all the bedtime stories I remembered. Pushing away the memories of my mom brushing my long hair and braiding it before I went to bed. My mind kept going to one, my mom telling me about the red-haired man whom I had to trust and tell all my dreams to, now I wondered why I had never met Professor Simpson before I went to university. In the story I was told of a pretty blond maiden who longed for her true love, he was the one who would sing her songs and mend her broken heart.

Then as if in a dream, I saw a young man, he was beautiful, and his hair looked like it was alive, a flowing waterfall that reflected all the colors in each strand. His eyes, so knowing, like he saw everything around him. My heart soared with love before I could even process the thought. His deep timbered voice captured my heart before I even understood the words he spoke. His lips were the perfect color while the barest hint of stubble graced his strong jaw. He was singing, as if just for me. He sang of wild roses, majestic mountains, and sparkling flowing mountain streams. I couldn't make out all the words and I was unsure of how this would help me break my curse. I shook my head, sadness crept in as I realized it was just a story. The feeling of loss stayed, and I felt my heart break just a little bit as the memory faded. Tyler, a voice echoed to me quietly. Tyler. Who was Tyler, and why did I know this story? How could it help me break the curse?

I reviewed all I could about that story. I remember my mom had made tea from rose hips and honey and told me it was the only way to make our lives healthier... I wondered if she had figured out some incantation to make us live longer. I reached the bench and sat down. I enjoyed the quiet stillness, the gurgle of the Water of Leith, and though overcast, at least it hadn't started to rain just yet. While I sat, I remembered another story, more of a song, I guess. It was about a young mom who lost her baby to faeries and had to perform various tasks to have the child returned to her. It was quite sad, and I wasn't sure why I remembered it now. The water seemed to beat with the tune in my head. I heard my mom sing the song and I hummed along. I wondered if my mom had put special herbs in the tea as she sang. I had forgotten that part until just now. I struggled to remember the words. I could see her dance and twirl in our kitchen she waved her wooden spoon around like she was a music conductor, and she sang loudly her voice carried in my memory.

Ho-bhan, Ho-bhan, Goiridh og

O

Goiridh og O, Goiridh og O;

Ho-bhan, ho-bhan, Goiridh og

O

Gu'n dh'fhalbh mo ghaoil's

Gu'n dh'fhag e mi.

The song or lullaby went on for many verses. The lady in the song still had not found her child and sang of many impossible tasks she had performed. I am not sure that the child was ever returned.

I wondered again at these memories, why was I having so many of them right now.

I looked over the lake and saw a young lady walking her dog, she glanced up and met my eyes, her eyes were a startling grey almost purple, she gave a little wave and kept on walking. I stood and started to make the long walk back to my house. I glanced over my shoulder and saw the woman looking at me, chills broke over my arms and I gave them a shake before I turned away and headed home. The garden path seemed a little darker than usual. I looked up and realized it must be close to dinner time. The afternoon had flown by fast as I recalled my mother's stories and songs. I quickened my pace to a slow jog and made it to the back of the house before the darkness enveloped me. I noticed the house lights had been turned on and I slowed to a walk. I enjoyed the early evening sounds as I rounded the corner to the front door. The smell of roasted pork and baked sweet potatoes greeted me as I entered the large front door. I removed my trainers and hung up my coat, then headed to the kitchen. Lisa and Enid were there laughing and cutting up vegetables for a salad, Mitch was setting the table.

All eyes turned to me as I walked in, "What can I do to help?" I asked.

Relief showed in their eyes and Lisa was the first to reply, "Everything's set. Could you get the milk from the fridge?"

We settled around the large wooden table ready to eat dinner, then my stomach gave a little grumble.

Enid looked over and gave a light giggle, "I guess breakfast was a long time ago."

I laughed "Yes, I suppose we should dig in before I die of starvation."

As I heaped the sweet potatoes onto my Scottish Thistle plate, I began to hum the tune my mom sang. Lisa looked up and remarked how it sounded just like my mom like her voice blended in with my humming. Conversation flowed about university classes, my plans for the near future, and how all three of them would help me in any way possible to break the curse surrounding me. The banter was light there would be no more heavy stuff tonight. All of us behaved and tried to believe that life could be normal for us. That we could go on like an unknown crazy person hadn't tried to hurt me with a fireball aimed at my head. Like I hadn't just met my long-removed grandfather. I didn't mention the chills I had gotten from the lady with the grey, purple eyes today by the river.

The dinner helped to release some tension, it was good to know I had the strength and trust of my adoptive family. As we cleaned up the kitchen, Mitch passed by me and patted my shoulder, which was like the biggest hug from him. I appreciated the gesture and smiled at him. Enid was being her usual bouncy self, telling funny stories about the people she met at the class library. She was never like this outside of the house. She had Lisa rolling her eyes and Mitch snickering. It was great, I almost forgot about my dilemma. As Enid told her little anecdotes I was reminded of the tall dark dark-haired nerdy guy who told me he had seen Enid in the library and was a bit concerned for her. As her last story ended with a quick giggle and Lisa laughed about boys, I asked Enid about the guy.

"I don't know who you're talking about Ava." Her brow scrunched up as she tried to think of who she knew.

I described him to her and still, she could not recall meeting anyone of that description. "Well, maybe we should go there tomorrow and see if he's around. After all, he seemed quite concerned about you." I wiggled my eyebrows at her and laughed.

The kitchen was back to its shining self quickly and the four of us went our separate ways in the large house. I climbed the stairs to my room and heard the murmuring of Lisa and Mitch. Their voices faded as the telly was turned on.

Enid was quiet as she climbed the stairs behind me. As I grabbed the door handle to my room, she said, "We will break this curse for you Ava, I promise you that."

I turned and smiled at her, "I hope so, goodnight, Enid."

"Goodnight," she replied and continued past me to her room.

I entered my room and as always, I was delighted by the calm that surrounded me. When we were seventeen, Enid and I decided we needed to update our childish rooms. Lisa and Mitch were helpful and accommodated our views, however, they did say no to a couple of ideas. I put on some relaxing music and grabbed my pajamas I headed into my bathroom. A long soak in the tub is what I needed to get a restful sleep. I plugged the tub and turned on the taps I walked over to the cabinet looked through my bath bombs and decided on a rose-blueberry-smelling one. Noticing my stash was getting low I reminded myself to go online and replenish them soon. Tossing the ball into the bath, I listened to the fizzy sound and grabbed one of my pink fluffy bath towels and a pink face cloth from the bathroom closet. Hanging the towel on the warming rack I stepped into the warm bubbly water, I placed my face cloth on the side of the tub. Grabbing a hair tie, I piled my hair up and sank into the rose-scented water.

After a nice twenty-minute soak my skin was pink and glistened. I dried off with my fluffy warm towel and spread rose-scented lotion on. Sliding into my pajamas, I walked to my bed and braced for the cool flannel, I turned off my lamp and snuggled into my bed. I closed my eyes and exhaustion took over. I fell into a much-needed deep healing sleep.

CHAPTER THREE

Enid

I left Ava at her bedroom door and headed to my room. The last five days had been hectic and emotional. When Ava found me in the linguistics library, I thought she was going to be so mad, I was so relieved to finally be able to tell her all my secrets, all except one. The fireball wasn't the first attempt to hurt her. It might have come right after the warlock, Majic, had left this earth but I'm pretty sure it didn't happen because he was gone. Unknown to Ava, there have been multiple poisoning attempts, and falls while hiking Arthur's Seat, the main peak in Edinburgh, even avoiding a shopping cart careening out of control at the market. Opening my bedroom door, I smiled, I loved this room, it was my favorite in the whole house. My four-poster bed with surrounding yellow lace and netting was the focus of the room, heavy wooden posts held the elegant netting. The white bedding was perfect with one large yellow rose embroidered on it. The room had plush white carpeting with yellow throw rugs strewn here and there. A heavy antique dresser and mirror, hand-sanded and refinished by my dad, warmed the decor enough. The old porcelain water bowl held all my scented candle wax. It gave off the sweet smell of vanilla. Instead of having one main light hanging from the center of the room, I chose to have little lights around the room go on with a main dimming switch. I had always had so much homework, that my mom had suggested I get a desk, chair, and work light in here for a kind of workspace. At seventeen I thought it was a bit much but now after three years of university, I could appreciate her suggestion. I loved the order at my desk the pens and pencils just so in their holders. The calculator set was a perfect tool for me. My laptop lay closed against the smooth wooden top of the desk. Walking to my adjacent bathroom, I appreciated the stark white walls and dark blue accents scattered around the space. Running warm water in the sink I wet one of the blue face cloths to wash my face. I appreciated the differences between Ava and myself, but I liked that neither of us wore much makeup. We had no time in our busy day to look at ourselves and decide what color eye shadow to wear. I ran a brush hastily through my long tangled curly hair and changed into my pajamas, slid into my slippers, and grabbed the housecoat that hung on the back of the door. Walking over to the window seat, I sank into the soft pillows, noticing again the stark difference of white and the navy blue of my robe. I looked out at the gardens below and then up towards the twinkling of the stars, beginning their night ascend. I slowly went over the events of the past few days.

 I was supposed to meet Professor, Craig Simpson, but he had run a bit late. So, I had picked up a book on Gaelic folklore, I still didn't understand how Ava was going to make a living with a Gaelic linguist major. I hadn't even understood her interest in the stuff. I kind of understood a bit better now. Books, numbers, tangible stuff, that's what made sense to me. I thought I would read a few stories and then I could at least have a conversation with Ava about it. I was shocked that I found it interesting, although I had still viewed it as fictional, just stories never holding any truth to them. I did know Professor Simpson was a warlock, I knew he wasn't fictional.

When we had started at the university, he had sought me out to explain their history. The McSymon family and my part in it. So, I had known the basics but until two nights ago I didn't know how important my whole family was to Ava. I also didn't know about Majic. I had been beside myself wondering how to protect Ava. I didn't know she was destined to die…and her children, was I going to have to raise them like my parents had raised her? Did it mean nothing to keep protecting her just to know at age fifty she would die, no matter what I did? And to top it off according to the legend Ava was going to have a girl child at the age of forty. We hadn't spoken of our future and kids. Everything up till now had been about school and grades and what professional careers we wanted. Occasionally throwing in a good-looking male to make our dream lives complete.

My thoughts casually slipped to Ian; he was so good-looking. He had a wild mane of burnished red hair and beautiful green eyes; with the longest lashes I had ever seen on the male species. With a family legacy behind him, he was free to pursue anything he wanted. He was an accomplished musician as well as a straight-A student in Business. He said he was going to run his family business in Glasgow after he had finished his wanderlust of touring. He was very driven and exactly the person I had been waiting for. I couldn't wait for him to meet my family now that I had told them about him. We had been casually dating for a year, both of us very studious about our schooling. Without realizing it we fell into this undefined relationship. When we had time, we ate together and spoke of our assignments, which had progressed to walks around some of the hidden gardens in Edinburgh. Holding hands, we had dashed in and out of rainstorms. We gently laughed at the tourists who tried to use umbrellas to stay dry. It was coming up to our second anniversary. His family obligations took him away on the breaks from school. He tried to call me every evening when his busy days were finished. He would tell little bits and pieces of the many employees whom he had spoken to that day and would tell me funny stories that had happened. He stayed away from talking too much about his family, saying he just preferred to keep them out of our relationship for as long as possible. I did learn they were important to the business community in Glasgow. I knew he had three brothers and two sisters, but he said they were all living their own lives and they usually just sent a text or a quick call on each other's birthday. I knew my mom and dad would love him. I hoped Ava would like him and appreciate how well we got on together. I gave my head a little shake and I turned my thoughts to the problem at hand, Ava, and her curse.

I had looked in the library countless times and hadn't found any mention of curses or how to break them. I counted myself lucky to have found anything at all considering Professor Craig hadn't broken the curse in his three hundred years of searching. Now that his friend Majic was gone, what on earth were we all going to do?

I couldn't just wait around for Ava to die. I looked over at my bookshelf and the many books I had lovingly bought or had been given over the years. It seemed one was not sitting right in its spot. Had someone been in my room lately? I knew it was going to just bother me if I didn't fix it, so I left my warm cozy nook and walked across the plush carpet to the shelf. The book kind of glowed, how was that possible? On closer inspection, I recognized it as the cookbook Avas' mom had given to me on my eighth birthday. I had always loved cooking and we had spent hours in her kitchen, cooking up pancakes, pies, and cookies. Ava and I happily ate everything we made and shared with our families as well. Every year from my eleventh birthday until I turned eighteen my mom had given me an envelope with my name written on it in lovely calligraphy. Inside would be a new recipe and a funny little story or memory from Ava's mom. I always made the recipe and shared it with my family and then carefully put the paper in my recipe book along with the message. I wondered if Ava had needed to read the stories and had forgotten to put the book away properly. I reached up to tap it into place and the book kind of jumped out at me. I glanced around quickly, no one was with me in the room. Feeling a little unnerved I tried to put the book in its place, but it wouldn't go in. That was weird, I thought. I took the book back to my desk, moved my laptop out of the way, and opened the book to the first page. Without touching it, the pages flipped open to the first recipe that Ava's mom and I had made. It was an easy biscuit with a chocolate chip recipe. Underlined with golden light were a few words. That hadn't been there before. Grabbing a pencil and a sheet of paper I wrote the highlighted words down.

New

Stir

½ cup

Well, that didn't mean anything, I turned the page and saw a few more words highlighted. I wrote them underneath the first three. And I kept going until I had gone through the whole cookbook. Closing the book, I glanced at my bedside clock, 3:01 in the morning! Feeling exhausted I looked down at the paper and decided sleep was more important. Ava and I could figure this out in the morning. Thankfully it was Monday tomorrow, and our classes didn't start till noon. I took the book across the room and put it back into its spot on the bookshelf, it just slid right into place this time. I turned off the lights and made my way to my bed. Gratefully I sank into the vanilla-scented sheets and drifted off to a troubled sleep where I dreamt of numbers, jumbled words, and green eyes.

CHAPTER FOUR
Professor Craig

I felt every bit of my three hundred and fifty years as I climbed the hill heading to the stone steps up to my professor's apartment. It was sparsely furnished and consisted of an open living floor plan. There was a large dining area and kitchen with modern appliances. I loved the new gas stoves. I especially liked hot showers. How had we lived without that marvel all those years ago? With a laugh and a tired sigh, I put my key in the lock and entered my space. Littered across my table were many books and papers. I should have put this onto a disk or drive for organization. Maybe later. I took off my walking shoes and put on my leather-soled slippers. I hung my jacket on the wall hook. Walked over to the bookshelf and grabbed a photo album then sat on the tan leather couch. My backside sunk neatly into the worn leather. I opened the pages, I marveled at the resemblances of the ladies, all my Edina ancestors over the years. All of them had variations of blond hair and blue eyes with that lovely kind of ethereal beauty surrounding them. The photos, all candid shots, reading books, playing musical instruments, learning jujutsu, that last one was of Ava. She had been concentrating so hard her forehead had a little wrinkle between her brows. I have always been around but never too close, fearful of breaking my heart just a little more every time a new baby girl was born. I hadn't been lying when I said Ava looked so much like Edina. I have noticed that Ava's attitude was a bit stronger. Ava liked to be right and always answered first in class. She would argue her point if the others in class disagreed. Ava was a born leader. I hoped as I had hoped for countless years, that she would be the one to break the curse on our family. Quietly I sighed and closed the book. Resting my head on the couch I removed my glasses and placed them on the table. I closed my eyes; a little rest was all I needed right now.

The evening light dimmed; I woke to the sound of someone knocking on my door. Still tired but feeling better I got up to answer the door. Replacing my glasses as I walked across the polished floors, I smelled the lemon from the cleaning solution the housekeeper used. I liked the housekeeping at this place. I opened the door. A young man with black-rimmed glasses was holding a thick book. I had a quick flash of recognition but shook my head, it couldn't be I silently told myself.

"Halo, can I help you?" I asked him.

"Halo Professor," he stated, "My name is Freedom Romany, I believe I have some new information on the curse that surrounds Ava MacSymon. I think you might need my help."

Not one to lose my dignity, I calmly stepped back and gestured for him to come inside. I closed the door quietly behind him and turned on the lights. I asked him for his jacket and hung it on the hook beside mine. Motioning him to follow I headed to the kitchen and grabbed the kettle. I placed it on the stove and asked if he wanted tea. He answered in the affirmative. I grabbed two cups from the cupboard and moved to the kitchen table, clearing away the books and papers I had scattered around to make room for the book he held tight in his hands. I asked him to take a seat while I got the teapot, and some chamomile tea bags along with a bit of honey. I noticed he nervously bit his lip, ran his hand through his dark hair and he seemed a little jumpy.

"Are you in danger?" I quietly asked him.

"I'm always in a bit of danger." The young man responded with a slight grin.

I poured two cups of steaming chamomile tea into mugs and added a good bit of honey to sweeten them.

"Well ok, Freedom, how is it that you know of this curse on Ava?" I started and then quickly added, "How would you know if I needed your help?"

After he laid the book on the table, I noticed that the binding was very old, the pages were yellowed with age. I was intrigued by what Freedom might know about the curse.

Freedom looked directly at me and without blinking said, "I am a descendant of Vano Romany, the gypsy who placed the first curse on your family. I mean you and your family no harm." He took a quick breath and continued, "There are a few gypsy legends of curses. Most of them are little hurts, nothing like a generational curse. Except this one, and it comes from my family. There are others in my family who would take this curse and cause more trouble for your family.

There are a few others who do not believe this wrong, done by our ancestor, belongs in the twenty first century. We didn't understand why Vano wanted a four-hundred-year curse." He briefly closed his brown eyes and continued, "I wanted to apologize to your family for this hurt and I wanted to help you try to change the outcome of the chant. I brought this grimoire filled with our history of chants, my family's grimoire, to see if it could help you in any way."

My eyes followed as his fingers gently, lovingly, grazed the old book. The cover was worn leather and appeared to hum beneath his hand. The golden etched letters seemed to shine brightly under the dim light of the overhead kitchen lighting. I knew I should feel a bit skeptical when listening to this young man, but he seemed genuine, I hadn't got a bad vibe from him in the minutes since he had entered my apartment. Just a quick flash of recognition. I noticed Freedom looked at me expectantly. I asked if I could have a look at the gypsy book of spells, or chants, as they called them. He gently turned the grimoire so I could look at it. The words were now right side up and he moved his hands down, so they rested gently on the table. He gave a little nod as if he were talking with himself but also to the book as if gave permission for it to do the right thing. Gingerly I touched the worn leather and felt a little vibration, I knew the book held magic, so I had anticipated the tingle. Opening the first page I could see what looked like a family tree, running my finger to the year 1880, I was shocked to see the gypsy's name, Vano, there. I glanced up at Freedom questioningly.

"The tree depicts the year a monumental chant was spoken, not the year of birth like a traditional family tree. The number beside the name is for the length of the chant." He explained to me.

I looked beside the gypsy's name and saw the number four

hundred. I looked at the other names and noticed far smaller numbers, two, six, ten, and so on. Not one of them bore a number higher than twenty-five.

"As I said before Professor, there are those in my family who did not think the chant needed to be that long. Others wanted to know why. Why it was such a long chant? It must have taken Vano a very long time to recover from such a chant. The chants usually required an exchange of life force or energy to be completed. There are many stories of the chant, but no one absolutely knows the truth. That's what I'm looking for, the truth, some closure for my family. There have been others that have come to you before but could not connect with you for some reason, or other. I hope that I'm the one able to figure out this chant with your help." Freedom took a breath and continued, "Please, could you look at page nine? Vano used this page to write down the chant he used, not everything is the same, but I do know of a lady in the old town, not far from here, who possibly would have everything we needed to break the curse."

Gently, eagerly I turned the delicate pages and counted to the ninth one. I closed my eyes as a pain so fierce touched my soul. I doubled over and held my chest. What had happened? How had my pain intertwined with this memory? I remembered how scared Edina had been, the day I met her. How she had hurled herself at me while she had tried to escape the gypsy, Vano. He had been so fierce that day. I never wondered why he was in town. The gypsy people mainly stayed out of it unless they were putting on a show. I never questioned why he had been willing to trade my beautiful wife for four animals. I was so smitten and knew I could glamour us so he would never find us. I felt his pain and beneath that, I felt his helplessness and something else, something I was not sure of. It was like pain but not quite. There was a little bit more anger and then the feelings were gone. I looked up at Freedom and he looked right back at me. I had hunched over the grimoire and was almost covering it with my upper body, I straightened up and looked at him again.

"How was that possible?" I asked. Still a bit stunned by the force of emotions the book had made me feel, I took a relaxing breath. "It was like I felt his emotions at the time he cast the chant. Do you feel that every time you open the book?"

Freedom smiled widely for the first time. "This was the first time that anybody else has ever touched the grimoire, who is not our direct lineage." He continued "It has been kept locked in a storage box for most of my life but a few days ago I had the strongest urge to go looking for it. I found it and easily opened the box; I have been carrying it with me ever since. I had it the other day when I went to the University of Edinburgh, I thought I could catch you after your last class, but you had already left. I wandered around the campus for a little bit and ended up in the class library. I knew I needed to talk to Enid first because she would never let anyone get near Ava. I caught a glimpse of her and was going to speak to her, but she left the building in such a hurry. I thought she might return, so I was just going to have a seat and look at the grimoire some more. A little later I saw Ava, she looked out of breath, I got up to speak to her and it was like someone else was speaking for me. My voice even sounded different to my ears. And I lied, I have never told a lie before, but I did, and I have no idea why I did it." His cheeks darkened with the telling of the truth, "Ava now thinks I am a student at the university and that I know Enid, whom I haven't even met yet."

Freedom and I talked long into the evening. He felt like a long-lost piece that fit into my life. Little puzzle pieces were beginning to join together. My family had consisted of females for so long that it was nice to talk with another male. I knew Ava's adopted family would love him like their own son.

I also knew the boy was telling the truth so I smiled at the end of our conversation and said, "I know the girls and their family would like to meet you, how about you accompany me to their house tomorrow? I'm moving a few things into a garden house on their property, and I could use a couple of strong arms to help me."

"Of course, I would help you move a few things, thank you for talking with me, it's getting late, and I need to get going now." Freedom gently turned the grimoire towards him and closed it with a soft thump.

I dared not ask but I couldn't see him leave here without asking, I turned my gaze from the old book to look at his face, "Might I keep the grimoire to read over tonight?" I held my breath and let it out slowly as I waited for his answer.

"I'm sorry Professor, the book must stay with me or a member of my family at all times. It hasn't been a minute away from one of us since the first page has been written." He looked gently at me and then at the leather-bound book and said, "If anyone could use and decipher the book right now, it's you, I'm sure of it, but again I'm sorry. I must take it with me tonight."

I nodded and told him that he was right, it belonged with him or his family. I could not imagine my spell book being read by anyone else either. He gently placed the old worn grimoire in a cloth bag which he then placed inside his knapsack. He tied it up and walked to the door, removed his jacket from the wall hook, and put it on. Slinging the bag across his shoulders he reached for the door, hesitated a second before he looked back at me.

"I appreciated your time tonight, Professor, let's get this figured out soon. I will be back here tomorrow to help move your things. I look forward to meeting Ava, Enid, and their family. It's been an interesting evening, I feel like I have known you forever, weird, isn't it? That feeling of familiarity." With a small smile, he opened the door and closed it quietly behind him.

Well, that was unexpected, it brought new hope to my otherwise dead-end search for a clue on how to break the curse. I wondered if I should start calling it a chant, no. It was a curse and after all these years I could still feel my heart break. I looked around and decided I should gather up my few belongings in the boxes I had kept. I had brought a bit more from my years at the University than I meant to. My favorite grey hoodie with the university name in Gaelic, Oilthigh Dhun Eideann, stamped onto the front. It was a hot seller; I noticed many students and quite a few professors wore them proudly around the school campus. I also had some new teacups and dishes. I wondered how long I would be in the cottage. I decided to phone the landlady and see how long I could keep the apartment. I hadn't signed on to instruct the same course next semester. I would wait to see how the next month went with the search for the cure. I'm buoyed by the fact that we now have a new lead and another set of eyes to help. Soon the rest of my belongings were placed by the door so that when Freedom came tomorrow, he would have no doubt what needed to be moved.

I had a good hour or so before I needed to get ready for bed, so I turned on my computer. I waited patiently while it booted up. Feeling a bit peckish I headed over to the fridge and gathered a few items to make a quick sandwich for dinner and brought it to the desk. I brought up the search bar and typed in *British Columbia, Canada*. Noticing the population, of five million, I wondered where I would start looking first.

My search to locate the hidden warlock had been a dead end so far. I looked at my wall map. The world map glittered with different colors each assigned to witches, warlocks, empaths, and various other magical or sensitive people. My warlock eyes focused on the country of Canada; the Province of British Columbia was highlighted but not narrowed down to which part of the province to look. I wondered why the warlock was in hiding. He hadn't cast a spell that I could detect. No ready-cooked food, no ever-full gas tank, not even a spell to win at a gambling establishment. How on earth did this warlock make a living? I knew my salary from the university barely paid the bills here in Scotland. I continued searching for possibilities and after about two hours of futile searching, I gave up and got ready for bed. I looked forward to meeting with Freedom and finding out what his grimoire had to offer. I had sent out a few emails to instructors in the BC area hopefully someone would have a clue who I was looking for. I washed and dried my dinner plate and utensils, wrapped them up in paper put them into the box with my other kitchen things, and placed the final box by the door. Ready for Freedom to carry out when he arrived in the morning. I locked the door and got into my pajamas, turned off the bright ceiling light, and turned on the bedside lamp. Picked up my novel and read a few pages then put it down. I turned off the lamp and fluffed my pillows. I closed my eyes and dreamed a dreamless sleep.

CHAPTER FIVE

Ava

I woke up, stretched my arms, and glanced at my bedside clock, eight o'clock. I had finally had a dreamless sleep. I would have liked to just curl up, pull the blanket over my head, and go back to sleep but, I knew I should get up and start my research. I also had to get through one more week of school. Final exams and then I could start my summer vacation. Squinting at the light coming into my window I sighed and threw back the covers. Might as well move it. Sliding into my slippers I headed into the bathroom and grabbed a fuzzy facecloth, ran the warm water over it, and washed my face. I felt much more awake.

Wandering lazily over to my closet, I chose a cute pair of pink shorts and a plain white T-shirt to wear. Who knew if I would have to run from flaming fireballs today besides, I needed a cute look to bolster my spirits. It would be hard to keep my mind on classes and exams when I didn't know who I would run into or if they would be a friend or a foe. I grabbed my white wallet and a pair of sunglasses from my dresser and headed downstairs. Everyone was already in the kitchen, Mitch was having a quiet conversation on the phone, Lisa was making scones and Enid was setting the table.

"Good morning, everyone," I smiled as I said it because today would be a good day. "I could whip up some oatmeal or cut up some fruit if it's needed?"

Lisa smiled and said, "Good morning yourself. I would love a plate of fruit and yogurt and if you have time to scramble some eggs that would be great. Enid has already cut the ham and it's warming in the oven with a nice honey glaze. I will set these in the oven, and we can start with the oatmeal its in the pot ready to serve."

Going over to the kitchen island I grabbed a plastic cutting board and a sharp paring knife. On the marble countertop, there are rhubarb, strawberries, and jostaberries along with tomatoes and cucumbers. Putting a large helping of yogurt in the center of the platter, I started chopping and piled fruit and veggies onto a serving platter. Arranging the fruit and veggies by color. Absently I wondered if I should go to culinary school then I reminded myself that I liked eating more than preparing and cooking the meals. I popped a strawberry into my mouth and smiled, it was like having a glass of juice every time you bit into the fruit. I loved that June fruit was so available, I missed the variety in the cold winter months. When the platter was full, I placed it in the middle of the table. I washed the cutting board and knife at the sink grabbed some eggs and cracked them into a white bowl. Hastily I whisked them until they were blended nicely. The eggs were scrambled quickly, and I sprinkled on some salt and pepper. The scones and warm ham had made the kitchen smell so good; my mouth began to water. I placed a few eggs on everyone's plate. Took the empty pan to the sink and washed it out then placed it on the drying rack. I sat at my spot at the large wooden table and spooned a large tablespoon of sugar into my bowl of oatmeal, put some fruit on my plate, and poured a cup of tea.

Mitch ended his phone call and said good morning to us. He said the housekeeper would head over to the garden house and prepare it for the Professor's arrival. The talk around the table was light and I enjoyed listening to Lisa and Mitch tease each other. We cleaned up that bit of breakfast and Enid walked over to the counter where the ham had been resting, Lisa grabbed the bowl of scones and some jelly. The ham looked so mouth-watering, and the left-over sweet potatoes melted in my mouth as I had my first bite. The scones were light and airy, and the jelly sweetened them just perfectly. I poured myself another tea and asked if anyone needed a refill. Only Mitch put his cup out. When we had eaten, and our bellies were full Mitch said he would finish cleaning up since he had missed the preparing. We got up and went our separate ways to start our busy day.

Enid told me she would be five minutes and then we would head out to the train station for school. I ran up to my room, brushed my teeth, and put my hair into a quick ponytail, grabbed a pink silk scarf and tied it around the hairband, added a little pink gloss to my lips, and grabbed my book bag. I took my white trainers out of the closet and bounded down the stairs to wait for Enid. She appeared within a minute, and we yelled out our goodbyes before we left the house. We would have quite a walk before we got to the train, and when I noticed Enid was being quieter than usual. I looked over at her.

I bumped her arm as we walked and said, "Hey, you're being awfully quiet this morning, everything ok?"

She looked at me with her big brown eyes and that's when I saw the excitement in them.

"Last night one of my books practically jumped off the bookshelf into my hands, it was the cookbook your mom gave to me for my birthday when we were kids. It wouldn't let me put it away, so I opened it and there were glowing words in it." She was talking so fast she had to let out her breath in a whoosh. It took me a minute to process everything she had just told me.

"Wait a minute." I stopped her. "What do you mean, *it* wouldn't let you put it away?" Who or what had been in her room last night?

"I'm not sure why I couldn't put the book away, it was like there was a cement wall that stopped the book from being put back into its spot." She replied. "Anyway, I took the book to my desk and when I opened it, it was like the words were written in gold lettering, not all of them, just random words in a jumble here and there."

I looked at her and waited for her to continue.

"You know every year on my birthday your mom made a gift for me. The envelopes with the recipe and a little story. Well, I looked through them all and wrote down the words that were glowing, I think your mom knew something to help with the curse. And this was her way of letting me have the clues to help you. I think she knew I would be the one to look out for you and that we would need this help once she was gone."

I asked if she had the list with her and she said of course she had it. We would meet at the library as soon as classes were finished today to figure this clue out.

We arrived at the train station and didn't have to wait long until it arrived. Once we were seated, I asked Enid to show me the list. Reaching into her backpack she pulled out her blue and yellow scribbler, inside were two sheets, she handed me one and said that that copy was for me. I looked at it and it made no sense to me. I glanced at Enid and was about to tell her so when she laughed.

"I know it looks like jumbled words, but there has to be a pattern and I will find out what it is." She smiled and her forehead scrunched up in determination.

I noticed the determined look on her face and knew she could do it. She loved a challenge, especially puzzles and word games. It was like my mom had been preparing her since she was little, just like she had been doing for me. We reached the campus stop and headed our separate ways setting a time to meet up at the front doors to the library after we were done classes.

The day sped by; I got my final exam prep sheets. Lunch had been a strawberry/banana smoothie. I wondered if I should grab a sandwich and then decided I would wait till I saw Enid and we could eat together. I made my way across the campus and smiled at people on the way to the library. There were so many students, professors, and tourists outside to enjoy the rare sunny day. I had a gut feeling we would find some answers today. So far, I only had questions that needed to be answered.

Walking toward the big main doors I ambled down the long hallway toward the class libraries I was pretty sure that was where I would find Enid. I was a little early. My gaze was drawn toward the hydroponic plants and there she was, soaking up the fake sunlight. She had her eyes closed and earphones on, she must be listening to music or maybe a history video. Enid had a lot of interests and she seemed to excel in all of them, except languages, although she understood five different languages, she was by no means an expert. I guess that's where my strong points lay. I am fluent in five languages and am still eagerly learning Gaelic and Turkish. Languages just seemed to come easily to me. I loved learning all the different sounds and putting it all together. Those were my kind of puzzles. As I thought about puzzles, I was reminded of the messages my mom had left Enid in her cookbook. I hoped Enid had found out more.

I gently nudged Enid's shoe with the tip of my trainer. Her eyes sprung open, and she sat up straight as though a shot of lightning had run through her. Whoa, I put my hands out palms upward to settle her down. She laughed and took off her headphones.

"Sorry," she said breathlessly, "I was listening to a scary movie on audiobooks."

She placed her headphones on the table beside her and got up reaching for her book bag. "Let's head over to the long table, to look at the annual recipe message."

I looked at her and grinned, annual recipe message? she had named the puzzle. I followed her over to the table and took a seat beside her. Enid took everything out and spread it onto the table. Her eyes sparkled as she started to explain.

"I thought your mom meant to message me with all these random words and as I tried to figure them out today, during my spare, I realized that I must have missed something. No matter how I turned the words, up, down, or horizontally, nothing made sense. So, I concluded that these must not be the only words left for me. I called my mom and asked her to grab the book off my shelf and help me out. She opened my book and started reading out the words that were highlighted. We quickly realized that the words she saw didn't match my words. So together we figured most of it out."

Enid's head snapped up and she quickly covered the pages before us as a shadow fell across the table. I looked up and met dark eyes covered by black glasses. It was the cute guy that had been looking for Enid the other day.

"Halo again." I smiled at the nerdy boy who stood before us clutching his knapsack like he was afraid it would be snatched by a thief.

CHAPTER SIX

Freedom

"Halo again," I replied to Ava. I stood looking down at the two of them. I had been waiting years for this and all I had said was, Halo again? Clearing my throat, I started again.

I looked at Ava and then at Enid. "Halo, my name is Freedom." He replied in a quiet voice. "I'm sorry to interrupt you, but Professor Simpson asked me to send you to his classroom. Would you mind if I walked with you that way?"

I watched as Enid quickly gathered up the papers and put everything back in her book bag. Ava took her phone out of her pocket and read a message from the professor. He explained that she could listen to me and head over to his classroom with Enid. I hadn't even heard the phone, of course, we were in a library, I'm sure Ava had turned it to silent before she had entered the building.

"I met you the other day, didn't I?" She asked me in her lilting Scottish accent. She had a gentle smile.

"I'm sorry but I'm afraid I led you to believe a lie that day." His cheeks darkened in shame. He noticed how they watched him struggle to tell them who he was and why he had lied to Ava earlier.

They walked out of the library, and Ava glanced at him. "Who are you, Freedom? Why did you lie to me?" she questioned him.

"It is a bit of a story, please don't be alarmed. I am a descendant of Vano, the gypsy who cursed your family." His silken voice murmured the words that should have scared her but instead, he saw his words intrigued her.

Enid gasped and lunged at him, with a wave and a mutter under his breath, he sidestepped Enid, and she looked like a statue mid-strike then in slow motion her fist swung towards where he should have been standing. Freedom gently held her elbow so she wouldn't lose her balance as her fist hit nothing but air. Ava looked quickly between Enid and I. Enid looked fierce and was ready to punch him again.

Ava's mouth opened then snapped closed. Shocked she said, "You're a warlock."

His eyes slid to Ava's as she spoke, and Enid's second punch hit him squarely in the jaw and twisted his head around.

"Stop this." He spoke firmly and deeply "I mean you no harm, I am here to work with you to break the chant."

Ava stepped between Enid and Freedom and said to Enid, "Hear him out, we need answers and if he can help us then let's listen."

Enid gave a little huff and picked up her bag, slung it onto her shoulders, and started towards Professor Simpson's classroom.

"I'm sorry about that." Ava apologized to me.

"It's ok, she's only doing her duty to you." I replied quietly.

CHAPTER SEVEN

Ava

We walked in silence the rest of the way. I knew Enid was still mad and would love to jujitsu her way across Freedom's face, but she was also a student and knew the answer to all this was to research and find a way to break the curse. By the time we reached the linguistics building, she had calmed down quite a bit. The professor greeted us with a wave and a smile.

"I see you've both met Freedom, so glad he's on our side. I learned so much by glancing at the grimoire that belonged to his family." The professor tsked under his breath as he looked at the red patch on Freedom's cheek and then turned to look at Enid his brow raised questionably.

Enid screwed up her face and let out a breath and muttered under her breath, "Like it's going to help, he's probably just looking for ways to curse her family again."

I looked at Freedom and noticed his cheeks go a shade darker. "Enid" I scolded, "let's hear him out."

She gave a quick jerk of her head, found a chair to put her bag on, and dragged another to plop herself into. Turning towards Freedom, Enid quietly said "Ok, Freedom, please tell us what you have to say. I hope it's informative and gives us answers rather than raising more questions."

Freedom took an old thick leather-bound book out of his backpack; he gently placed it on the table in front of us. I marveled at the age of it. I could tell by the front cover it had to be a couple of hundred years old. He started to open the pages; then he began to tell a tale.

His melodic voice seemed to bring the images to life. In my mind, I could see a large dark-haired, dark-skinned family laughing around a campfire, their teeth white in the darkness when they opened their mouths to laugh. Every eye was on the small man dressed in flamboyant colors; his boots tinkled with the sound of the bells tied to his boots he was telling many stories. I could almost feel the love emitting from the small boys and girls at his feet, the loving eyes of a beautiful woman wearing a white and red dress. Her beautiful hair piled loosely on top of her head with a bright yellow flower. The stem seemed to weave and grow through her dark locks. A babe in her arms nestled lovingly like she never wanted to leave.

The picture changed to a traveling band of gypsies, a caravan of carriages, about thirty of them, following one another. Angry villagers yelling obscenities at their backs. A baby crying, dogs barking, and bells rang from their footwear as every step took the gypsies further away from the villagers.

The story told was of happier times at each stop, a welcoming community happy to have the performances of the gypsies. Sometimes they stayed for one month and sometimes it was much longer. Eventually, though, the men of the villages they were visiting would charge the gypsy men with some criminal activity, and again and again the gypsies would have to move on. Sometimes, a young male gypsy would fall in love and the girl would leave her family to travel with her new family, the weddings were fabulous feasts with big dances and stories. The girls would bear children and the gypsy clan would grow bigger. They were a loving family.

In between the good times, there were also stories of death, of the elderly, and of sicknesses that could not be cured. The gypsy man aged through the story and loved with his whole heart, his family members adored him and learned all the stories and then each one would write a story in the big leather-bound book that was always a part of their time together. Every wedding, every birth, and with sadness every death had been lovingly recorded by the Gypsy man's pretty wife, and at her death he took over the writing. The stories changed though, they no longer were about happiness, they were about death and anguish, the children who had lovingly followed him now looked at him with skittish eyes, only the older ones felt his pain and the anguish at his wife's death. They also took to telling harsh stories to their young siblings and then their children. This included the man who sat with us, Freedom.

He stumbled a little bit when he told us this part of the story, but he continued with a deep calming breath.

He started with why Vano's wife died. She had been heavy with child, and the community happy at their fortune, failed to notice her heavy weight gain, swollen legs, and feet, and how her hair, usually radiant with pregnancy, was lifeless and dull. At the end of her term, she was bedridden, hurt with every movement, and waited anxiously for the birth of their child. No longer able to keep any food down she took to just sipping water. The gypsy man was in anguish watching his love, who kept everyone together and happy, wither away while awaiting the birth of their child. As a last effort to get her to eat the gypsy man went to town to buy a chicken, using his wits he thought he could double his money to get a goat so the children of his family could have milk to drink as well as the newborn. He feared his wife would be too weak to feed another child. He was headed to the town center when he heard a few men laughing down a quiet dark alley. He hoped to find a drunken man willing to part with a few gold pieces, so he darted into the alley and faced the laughing men. They were taller and broader than him, but he knew he had the smarts to beat them. With a flourish and a smile, the gypsy man introduced himself and asked about a game of chance. The men, heavily into their bottles, agreed and a tall blond giant with piercing blue eyes seemed the most eager to bet. He graciously shared his drink with the gypsy man and bet heavily. He was losing his money and his temper as well. The gypsy man knew he had to leave with his winnings as he noticed the blond giant swat the man beside him as he lost his money. Rising to leave, the gypsy man gathered his coin into the purse that hung on his belt. Quietly the men watched him, eyes blurry with drink, each quietly wondering how the gypsy had taken all their coin. The blond giant also stood and quietly told the gypsy man he had one more bet to make. Swaying, he bet his oldest daughter for the gold in the gypsy man's pouch. Quickly the gypsy man declined but the blond giant would not take no for an answer and the gypsy man sat back down. The game began and, in the end, the gypsy man won. In a rage, the blond man grabbed the gypsy and held him up furiously blinking his eyes as if he could stop the spinning. He dropped the gypsy and staggered to the house. Not knowing what to expect, the gypsy turned to leave but the other men blocked his way. There were loud angry words that came from the house. His eyes were wide as he turned to look at the doorway, he saw the blond giant come out of the house with a young maiden. Her long beautiful blond hair was uncombed and tangled about her slim shoulders, her clothes made of harsh linen and her feet bare. The blond giant threw the girl at the gypsy man's feet and told the girl child to obey him and never show her face in his home again. The gypsy was aghast that this man would treat such a child so harshly. He quickly thought of his children at home waiting for him to bring them a goat and a chicken to eat. How could he feed another mouth especially with a sick wife? But he couldn't leave this innocent girl with this man either. He quickly grabbed the girl and helped her to her feet. She was crying and as she looked at him, he was startled by the frail beauty, he looked into her tear-filled eyes and turned her towards the alley. The drunken men had moved aside, and he noticed their glassy eyes fill with lust at the girl. She was a bit older than he had originally thought but still to young for these drunken sots. He grabbed her arm and started towards the city. He was still in need of a chicken and goat. His mind raced, he thought she might make a good wife for his son. She could look after the new babe while his wife could regain her health. His mind was made up and he asked the girl her name. She refused to answer, she stumbled, he helped her gain her balance and kept a hold of her arm. Quietly she cried and as she stumbled again, he let go of her arm. Quick as lightening she darted to her feet and ran towards her home. Her fathers' friends laughed as they grabbed her, she wiggled and tried to get away, they slurred and swore at her, tearing one piece of her dress from her arm. The gypsy man walked towards the group and tried to help the girl. Unknown to him his belt had come loose, and a few coins spilled out. The blond giant returned and clubbed the drunken pair in the head and the girl ran towards her father. She threw her arms around his waist and begged him to let her come home. He unwrapped her arms and sternly shoved her toward the gypsy, telling her to never return to his home. She crumpled to the ground and wailed that she would be better and look after the family. The blond giant turned and walked away from her and he didn't look back once. The gypsy man gently helped the frail girl up and was about to tell her everything would be ok. She would be welcomed into his family. She removed her hands from her face and slapped his face as hard as she could then turned to run towards town. The gypsy man was stunned to have been on the receiving end of such treatment, he just wanted to help her. He rubbed his face where it stung and raced after her, coins falling from his pouch as he ran. The tinkling of his boots masked the sound of coins as they fell to the ground. He rounded a corner and ran into an active centre. There were people selling their food and travellers looking to supply their travels. He noticed the girl then, she had hidden behind a young man, tall with red hair. The young man yelled at him to leave her alone or he would report him to the Chancellor. The gypsy told him she belonged to him. He told the boy that he had won her in a game of chance from her father. They would leave the town tomorrow and he wasn't going to leave without her. The young man defended the girl, she was still whimpering quietly behind him. He asked what the price was to keep her. The gypsy man decided then that another mouth to feed would be to much, so he asked for a sheep, two chickens and a rooster. That would help his wife gain strength, eggs and milk would help feed his family for awhile. It was what he had come to town for and so he bargained with the young red-haired man, he realized that his money pouch had torn and all the coins he had won that day were gone. The young man agreed to the terms, and they made a deal to meet at the town gate the next dawn. The gypsy looked once more at the girl, nodded his head and with a swirl of his arms, the fabric of his clothing billowing out he disappeared with a bang. The gypsy, Vano, was at home once more, he pleaded with his wife to live. To see the child in her womb, grow and thrive within the family. The wife nodded that she would wait till the babe was born. She sipped at bits of water and ate a few berries to keep her strength. Her children came into her room throughout the night to see her, touch her hair, now faded, and tangled. They whispered stories to her, told her of their days. They hid their anguish at each visit, and they watched her wither away from them hourly. Vano stayed with his cherished wife, he had told her of the day he had had and the lovely young girl that had almost come home with him but that he had traded her in a most fortuitous trade. Meat, eggs, and milk for the family. They would be well taken care of for the winter months the new babe included. The newly born babe would benefit and grow strong from the goat's milk. He told her how she would gain the strength she needed to deliver the babe into his arms. They would stay put and travel to the next city as soon as she was strong enough to move. He placed another blanket on her as she shivered from the cold earthen floor. Vano held her hand and sung songs to her until the night changed to light. The morning eerily, quiet and calm just before daybreak. He made sure his lovely wife was comfortable and whispered that he would be back as soon as he could. He carried his boots outside of the caravan and sat on the steps. The tiny jingle of bells carried around the encampment as he wrapped the leather around his feet. He stood and looked around at the wild overgrowth of heather. The light sway of the flowers beckoned him to run his hands across their purple tops. His steps were lighter than they had been in weeks, he set out towards the gate to the town. He quickly came up to the gate and looked around. He was alone, the young red-haired man had not shown. His fists closed in rage. He looked up to the sky and saw blackness instead of the brilliant rays of sunlight creeping across the fields touching all the waving heather, their faces turned up to catch the light. The sunlight touched the far cliffs highlighting their red rock and glinted like diamonds. The grass usually so green, was now yellowing with the coming winter. The town, however, was covered in darkness, the dark clouds rolled fast just waiting to burst with rain and lightening. The thunder rumbled ominously seeming to come from deep within Vano as his eyes opened, he saw nothing but rage and hatred. His eyes changed color, silver with flashes of purple lightening in place of the irises usually there. Disbelief in the knowledge that his wife was dying as he was here waiting on an untrustworthy red-haired boy. His grief clouded his mind, the emotions rolled through his body, and he let out a cry. A single tear fell from his eye, the heavens seemed to open, and a droplet of rain let loose from the stormy clouds. Just one, one lonely tear. Then Vano saw the boy and behind him he had brought a goat, two chickens and a rooster. Glaring at the clouds Vano tried to undo the storm he had created and bit by bit the storm receded. However, there had been the one rain droplet. He hoped it wasn't enough to harm them. He walked toward the young red-haired man and took the rope guiding the goat and the chickens the rooster followed behind. He took out a pouch from around his neck and muttered a few words and took a healthy swig. That was all he could do, hopefully it would be enough to save the townsfolk from the raging storm he had started. He never looked backward as he proudly walked back to his waiting family. He had done everything he could to save them. He hoped it would be enough. It was not long until he arrived home, his oldest child met him and helped him home with the newly acquired animals. A joyous smile spread across his dark face. They would all be okay. He had made a good trade. They would be fine; the babe would be born, and his wife would heal and grow strong once more. The children had made a rickety fenced in area to house the animals while he had gone to town. The little children were eager to pet the goat and had named her, Trina. She seemed to be a happy goat, going from child to child and butting her nose into their outstretched hands. Their laughter at her antics warmed Vano's heart. His wife seemed to have perked up at his arrival and wanted to see his new farm animals. Her belly swollen with their unborn child she was helped to the doorway to see little Trina and the chickens running in the little space made for them. She smiled and watched for a few minutes, but that effort seemed to tax her strength and she was helped to bed shortly after. That night they sat together by a campfire and Vano told them a new story, one they hadn't heard before.

It was about a golden-haired girl with eyes the colour of blue cornflowers. Her skin smooth and white as porcelain, her cheek bones high and her nose a perfect little button. Her family were unable to care for her, but she had found true love with a strong red-haired boy who was kind, and faithful. Their love was said to span lifetimes, they would forever find each other throughout time. They would raise a long line of strong children who looked like a mixture of them both. They would walk the earth many times and each time, their souls would find their way together. His children smiled at the blissful love story hoping they too would find their own true loves. As night wore on Vano blessed each child good night and made sure the fire was out. They climbed into their carriages and found a blissful sleep each one eager to drink the milk that Trina would produce for the morning. They fell asleep with light hearts and smiles on their lips. Vano, tired from his vigil by his wife's bedside the night before, kissed her gently on the forehead. Happy to feel it was cool and not ravaged by fever. His light touch made her open her eyes, the dark brown seemed to envelop his heart. His love, how he loved her so. She would be ok. He got her some water and watched while she took a few healthy swallows. She told him she loved him and how he looked after all their family. They all loved him. Her breathing turned regular and soon she rested peacefully. He removed his clothing and lay down beside her bed. He gently held her hand in his as he finally fell into an exhausted but happy sleep.

I saw the feelings in everyone's eyes as they looked at me and waited to hear the end. The professor was intrigued by the story. He remembered this story, but only from his perspective, he had not thought of the family the gypsy had had to take care of. Enid's eyes were full of suspicion and doubt. She had her job of protecting Ava to consider and I was still the enemy in her mind. Ava looked at me with unshed tears shining in her eyes. It made them seem even bluer. My heart skipped a beat as she looked back at me. It seemed an eternity passed before we broke eye contact. The professor cleared his throat and passed a tissue box to Ava.

"I suppose over the years I have thought about the gypsy and what had happened when he left the village gate all those years ago. But I was too wrapped up in my life and in making Edina happy. Then I tried to make my daughter happy and then my grief wrapped me in its steel grip, and I didn't think at all for many many years. I hadn't thought about the gypsy until he appeared to me so many years later." Professor Craig looked at me with sadness in his eyes. "I am very sorry that I took advantage of your family, Freedom. I hope that we all will be able to forgive and work past this lesson that has taught us so much. To appreciate every living thing on the earth and heavens and everything in between."

My heart seemed to lighten with his words. I had waited for years to find this man and break the curse on Ava. I needed to finish my side of the story, so he knew without a doubt what he and his love had done to our family the night they stole away from the village. They had left my family devastated. Our main reason for living, our mother, grandmother, sister, aunt, and cousin had been taken from all of us.

"Thank you for your words, Professor," I looked at him with tired eyes and said, "I'm afraid our story doesn't end there."

"Of course, not" Enid huffed out.

Her accusing eyes hadn't softened with the story of my parentage or of the hardship we would suffer at the hands of the very man sitting across from me. I had nothing but truth for her and after knowing her history I hoped she would let me into her world. It was like she was a planet all her own. She looked like a faerie with her dark hair coiled up on her head. My heart skipped a little beat as I watched her tongue dart out to moisten her ruby-red lips. I had to stop that; this was a much bigger deal than any of them knew. I glanced back to Ava, and I knew I had to help her stop the curse, I couldn't stand by and watch this young witch fail time and time again. She would live her life all the while knowing that it would be cut short because of something my ancestors had done. This girl, this life, this family had to continue. I had had a dream and knew this chant had to end in this generation or a world event unlike we had ever seen before would start. The anger Ava had inside her was unfathomable. I wondered if she was even aware of it. Did anger boil inside her, did it just sit steaming until someone set it off? Had she hurt people without knowing she could, did she even realize how powerful her anger could be? Questions churned in my mind, I couldn't help myself, I wanted to know everything about her.

Looking down at the old leather-bound book on the table I saw it give a little quiver, it was unsettled here in their presence. It had been gone too long from the family. Quietly I resumed the story, I hoped we could figure something out before bad things started to happen. I knew my cousins were around here somewhere. They had masked themselves, but I could faintly feel their presence.

I started where I had stopped, and three sets of eyes looked up at me expectantly.

"In the morning when Vano checked on his very pregnant wife, he rejoiced at her pinkened cheeks, gone was the pale color and sunken cheeks. This was the woman whom he loved dearly, her eyes were open and sparkled with life. They clearly looked at him and her lips turned up in a loving smile. She asked for water and then wanted to get up and see her children. Vano happily got up and pulled on his britches. Then put on his wrap-around shoes with the jingling bells. He leaned over and helped her sit up comfortably, he placed a pillow behind her back and went to get her a drink of water. He thought he could do better, so he went to get milk, from the goat, for her and the babe in her belly. He grabbed the bucket which hung off a rail around the animal pen, he opened the makeshift gate. Called gently to the goat and watched her walk slowly toward him. He rubbed her head and fed her some grass talking gently to her, he touched her neck and her back and rubbed her back legs. She turned and bleated and bumped her head against his arm, saying thank you to him. He squatted down beside her and tried to milk her but was surprised when nothing came out. He spoke soothing nonsense words to her, he begged for milk to feed his family. After a lengthy time, he gave up. He patted Trina on her head and walked back to the caravan. He brought his wife some water and held the glass to her lips as she drank deeply, he promised her some milk after dinner. He heard his children rise and went to help them on their way to finish their daily morning chores, his oldest girl stayed behind to look after her mother and the youngest children. Throughout the morning the boys wandered into the animal pen and tried to get eggs from the chickens or milk from the goat, but every time they left empty-handed. The gypsy was getting worried again. Why were the animals not producing for his family?

Lunch was a lively affair his wife smiled happily at everyone and hugged all the kids, the younger ones snuggled up on her lap as close as they could get with her burgeoning belly in their way. Vano lovingly listened to them all talk and appreciated how blessed he was to have such a family. The day wore on and the chores were all complete for the night their dinner had been noisy and filled with laughter. It had been sparse but filled them all enough. He went outside with his oldest son to check on the animals before they turned in. The goat lay on its side and bleated sadly, the rooster and the chickens were gone, and there were three piles of feathers in the middle of the pen. Hastily, Vano went to the goat, he thought that it had somehow eaten the birds and now had a stomach ache. His heart was heavy he knew that that wasn't the problem, he knew he had made a bad deal with the red-haired young man. He approached the goat and it looked up at him with sad eyes and then disappeared with one last bleat, the rope lay coiled and forgotten on the barren ground. Vano let out a howl and fell to his knees, his son touched his shoulder and worried at the shudder that ran through his father. Vano placed his head in his hands and cried. What would he do? He was angry, the boy had lied, and stolen. He would get the girl back and trade her again. He stood up wiped his eyes on the back of his hands and looked at his oldest son.

'No word about this to the family, I will deal with the traitor myself on the morrow.' Vano said as he turned to leave the empty animal pen.

Vano walked back inside the caravan and put everyone to bed, all the while his mind made plans to find the traitor and make things right with his family. Vano's mind was spinning. Gently he took his wife to bed, doused the candles, and tried to get some sleep. The following hours, before the sun could break the horizon Vano walked furiously toward the city. He was eager to find the red-haired boy who so traitorously had traded him the animals for the lovely young blue-eyed girl. He entered the city through the gate and headed towards the center of town where the big church stood. The church was undergoing some renovation work and was unoccupied right now. Vano searched the city streets up and down all day long but to no avail. The young red-haired man and the pretty blue-eyed girl were nowhere to be found. He tried to remember the girl's father, yelling at her and the words he spoke. Her name. He couldn't quite remember. He stopped at the young girl's house and spoke to her father. He tried to make peace with the man, but the man said she was his problem now. And turned and walked away. Vano had to pass through the center of town to get to the gates and as he walked, he thought to stop in at the big church. Even though it was being fixed right now he thought there might be a priest around to give him prayer for his family. As he walked through the town, he noticed the vendors loading or unloading their wares to be sold in the market and he grieved that he had no money to purchase a real goat. He slowly trudged up the stone steps of the church, his head hung low. He pulled on the heavy wooden door and entered the cool stone church, stopping to look around for anybody. He quietly asked if there was a priest in the building and received no answer. He slowly walked down the aisle between the rows of wooden pews running his hands on the smooth polished wooden benches. He noticed a piece of cloth lying in one of the corners and bent to pick it up, it was the same scratchy fabric the blue-eyed girl had been wearing as she had run through the town trying to get away from him. He heard a noise and looked up and saw the priest enter from a back door. He tucked the piece of cloth in his pocket and went to talk to the man. The priest looked up and made the cross sign and asked how he could help the gypsy man standing before him. Vano explained all that had happened and asked for the priest's help in locating the two young people and asked for a prayer for his sickly wife. The priest shook his head and told him he had married the two the day before and that they had packed up and left that day. He had no notion of where they were going or how they had left and was sorry for the trouble that he had gone through. He offered to pray for him and his family.

Defeated Vano walked slowly out of the church and back to his caravan. He knew his wife needed food and water. What would happen to them now? They must pack up and move on. His sadness rapidly changed to anger. He cursed at the turn fate had given him. He cursed the young red-haired man and the pretty blue-eyed girl. He swore to get revenge.

Upon returning to his caravan, he noticed his children all clustered outside, but his oldest son and oldest daughter were nowhere to be seen. He then heard the younger children singing. It was a song he had heard many times before over the years. It was the song that they sang to welcome a new birth into their family. He walked rapidly. The children moved to let him inside the caravan. Inside he saw his son holding his wife. And at the end of the bed. His oldest daughter was holding a little pink bundle. The baby had been born. His wife lay gasping for breath. She was crying silent tears and asked to see her baby. He walked quickly to his daughter and kissed her head then he wrapped his new daughter gently in her blanket and brought her to meet her mother. She lovingly touched the girl with her hand and smiled at her. She ran her hand over the babe's black silky hair and named her Rose. Vano looked down at Rose and brought her to her mother's lips for a kiss. She handed something to Vano. It was a locket on a long thin leather string.

'For Rose' she said.

Vano handed the little girl to her oldest sister tucked the locket into the blanket and asked her to clean her and bring her back to feed. His son and daughter left to share the news with their siblings. Vano gently took his wife's hand in his and told her how beautiful she looked and thanked her for the precious gift she had given him. He told her he was sorry for not being there when she needed him and promised he would not leave her again. She smiled and said she had loved him from the day they met and had been happy every day since. Then she told him she had to go. It was her time to travel the stars, but she would be shining for him until the day he joined her. Tears filled his eyes and ran down his weathered cheeks. He would miss her so. Quietly he kissed her hand and her forehead and bade her safe travels. He told her he loved her and would care for their family for as long as he could. She smiled at him and closed her eyes; one lone tear fell from her eye to land on his hand. He held her for as long as he could, to ease her way on her next journey.

His oldest would be coming back in with the new babe, Rose, and so he stood up. He pulled the blanket that was covering his wife up over her head and turned away. There would have to be preparations made for his wife's travels. He heard as his oldest daughter gasped and muffled a cry. She cried quietly so she wouldn't disturb the sleeping child she carried in her arms. They turned and walked out of the caravan to let the rest of the family know. The next week was a blur of preparations and visitors, many left food for the family. Others offered to complete chores, some asked where the animals were. The rickety fenced-off area was completely bare now; the feathers had long gone with the wind. There was a feast and mourning songs were sung. There was also some laughter at the antics his wife had gotten into when she was younger, those stories brought sad smiles from him. The days turned into weeks and then months, the little girl, Rose, grew steadily and wormed her way into her father's heart. Every day the pain eased around his heart, and he started to take care of his family once more. The quiet evenings began to fill with giggles from the young children. They moved around quite a bit, Vano could never sit still it seemed. The children took on more chores to compensate for the absence of their beloved mother. Vano seemed to dry their tears less and less as the months went on. The nights were the hardest, sometimes he cried silently into his wife's pillow, missing the scent of her, missing her touch, her soft voice, even when she chided him for not listening to her. His heart ached and yet he had to continue, for their children. His oldest son had made a trade to get a cow and they had had nice fattening milk for the whole winter, the reason Rose had grown so fast. His little Rose. He loved her a bit more than the others, she was his last gift from his wife, their last child. He held her more than he had his other children. His oldest daughter had been raising her as her own. His growing family kept getting larger, his older son had taken a wife, and they would soon expect their own child. His first grandchild. He missed his wife when he thought this, they should have had years to celebrate the new additions to the family. The younger girls already had young men asking to woo them, it wouldn't be soon, and they would leave to join the boys' families, or they would choose to stay with him and raise their children among them. Life would carry on. The days turned to weeks and then months and soon years had passed by. Vano still grieved and sometimes became angry, the children who had stayed with him all his life now worried, this was not the man who had raised them with love, laughter, and song. They heard him talking late into the night when no one was around.

There was once a large bonfire and they heard him chant nonsense into the darkened skies overhead. He slept later and later in the day only to keep awake late into the night. Even little Rose, who looked so much like her mother, couldn't wake Vano from his stupor. One night she walked out to the bonfire and curled up on her father's robes while he was yelling nonsense into the fire, begging for his wife to return. His oldest daughter was frantic when she awoke to find Rose's bed empty. She ran out and found them both asleep by the still-burning coals. Her father's face had been streaked with tears and little Rose was holding his hand. Rose's delicate white skin seemed to reflect the glowing embers on her flushed cheeks. Her dark curls framed her elfin face. The sister knew behind the long lashes that graced her sister' cheeks were eyes so wonderfully brown, like the shimmer of fresh ground coffee with just a hint of cream. She was a lovely child. She roused them awake and told them to get inside and clean up for breakfast. Then she doused the embers and carried the robe inside and hung it in her father's cupboard.

Little by little the roles had changed in the caravan, the oldest daughter had begun to take care of everyone the way her mother had. The son became the man of the troupe, and his wife was the second in command with his sister. The family continued. They tried to help Vano, they fed and clothed him, while he wandered around looking for any sign that his wife would come back. He tried to tell his stories around the campfire at night, but they always ended in death and heartache. The kids thought it would help him if he talked about his loss and so they let him continue. The stories changed from being loving and kind to stories of hurt, humiliation, and revenge. Vano plotted his revenge for years and he had researched many curses and found that there would be nothing bad enough for the red-haired man and the pretty blue-eyed girl who had fooled him and were the reason his wife had died.

His children grew weary of him as the years went on and they listened to him curse the two who had cheated him and his wife of many years together. They watched while he furiously wrote notes in the family chant book, scribbling and rewriting until one day he told them he was finished. They all breathed a sigh of relief, hopeful the grief that had held him in its grip for so long had been finally released. Vano eventually smiled again and went to work sporadically. He earned money for the special ingredients he needed for a special chant; he told them. The kids were more than happy to help and were happy to have their father back. Then one day he just disappeared from their lives, he was gone for weeks. Upon his return he looked younger than he had in years, his clothing was neater, his beard trimmed, and his eyes brighter and focused. He stayed with the caravan helping to raise the kids and grandkids and then his great-grandkids.

Every ten years he disappeared for a month or so and told the family that he was just taking a break. They believed him, he always came back refreshed but soon he started to look younger than his oldest son and daughter. They wondered where he went but they were consumed with raising their kids and grandkids and so never thought too much of their fathers' disappearing acts. Time went on and everyone aged except him. One by one his children left this earth to join his wife, their mother, he cried as this happened but then remembered his revenge and how he still blamed the family who had conned him for the animals needed for his wife's survival.

Vano took special care with his last child, Rose, she had grown to be a duplicate of his wife, and her eyes sparkled warmly when she laughed. Her heart was so giving, and she treated him fairly. She even gave him trouble when he needed it. He taught her all the stories from the worn leather chant book, she knew them almost all by heart. She was angry when he told her the story of her birth and how she had lost her mother. He rightfully told her who had taken her away from them and their family. How it was up to them to make sure they paid for their greed. Rose knew the long chant by heart. Rose would know how to keep the curse going after he had finally exhausted his time here on Earth. He knew it would be soon, but he had no idea exactly when he would leave this earth and join his lovely wife and his children.

He replayed the last time he saw the red-haired man; it had been many years ago, at a funeral. The man's girl child was being buried, she was old enough to have had a child, another girl, she had the same blond hair as her mother. Her eyes had been swimming with tears. Vano had felt a little grief for her but then he looked at the man beside her, it was the same red-haired man who had taken his beloved wife from him. His grief surfaced again as it had every few years. Vano had made the trip to see several of these funerals. He saw the grief, the pain, etched in their eyes. He thought he would feel complete, vindicated. He was wrong. He felt nothing but rage, still, after all this time.

One time the red-haired man had caught him watching a funeral. Vano and a group of men had traveled to Edinburgh to secure work for the winter. Vano smiled at the red-haired man and asked how it felt to lose everyone he loved. He had sneered and laughed as the man had bowed his head. He couldn't help himself; he told him then what he had done all those years ago. The chant he had used on his family, it would last forever, never undone if his family continued. Just long enough that they all bonded and imagined long futures together, the girl would die, repeatedly. Before he could hear what, the red-haired man replied, he swirled his capes and disappeared. He went and hid to be sure the man couldn't find him and his family. He continued to watch them closely, unsure what the man would do now that he told him what had happened to his family. He saw the man enter universities throughout the world looking into curses and how to break them, but he knew he wouldn't find anything. Vano continued with his teachings to Rose and her little son. He had kept Rose young like himself, she wanted to stay with him, they raised her son together teaching him the chants from the book. He was different though, kinder, the family catered to the child, and his older cousins took him in when he needed a break from the teachings his mother and grandfather pushed him to excel at. They had named him Fredric, they raised him to his teenage years and then one day he left with no warning. His cousins told them that he went to find himself, he wanted to know more of the world, go to school with other people. He wanted friends who he could laugh with, free time to engage in other pursuits rather that look and remember chants from an old dusty chant book. He had learned all he could from the book and now he wanted his own life. It hurt his mother, Rose, and his grandfather, Vano, when he left. He would return when he learned all he could about the outside world, away from the tight knit family he had been raised in. Fredric knew his mother and grandfather would still be younger than their siblings and probably even his cousins. He had time to learn and grow in society. He left with nothing, but his clothes and a good luck charm handed down to him from his grandmother, a locket wrapped in a long strip of leather.

Freedom opened his hand and showed it to the people seated at the kitchen table.

"My name is Fredric Black, but everyone has called me Freedom since I could remember. And that is my story. I wanted to know why my grandfather cursed your family for four hundred years. I wanted to know how to break the chant and I needed all your help to complete my mission." I looked at each of them meeting their eyes, Enid's were still full of anger and doubt, Professor Craig looked sad, but Ava's were glittering with determination, she and I were on the same page. Her to save her life and her families lineage and myself to heal, to understand and to forgive. I had finally found them all and they knew most of the truth, this chant had to be broken the world depended on it.

CHAPTER EIGHT
Enid

I watched the warlock, Freedom or Fredric, whatever his name was as he wove his tale. The stories he had been raised to know, based on hatred and grief. I hadn't known the professor very well personally, but he genuinely seemed to be the nicest person I knew besides my parents. Could he really be the person solely responsible for the death of this gypsy family? Had his blind love for Ava's great great great grandmother been the cause. I couldn't believe a love like that could exist, I thought of Ian in the moment and then pushed him to the back of my mind. I had the ability to sense liars, it had helped a lot when I had been trying to look out for Ava. Gradually as the years passed, I had learned to trust this instinct and my other powers. I was not a witch or anything, but I could heal Ava, and I learned early on that anything that hurt her had the ability to transfer to me. The first time it had happened was when Ava had fallen off her bike and broke her arm, my mom had been watching and saw me fall to the ground immediately after Ava started crying. She ran to me and told me in private that I would be ok. Ava and I had both gotten matching casts for six weeks that spring. Since then, my mother had helped me care for my best friend.

My mom's best friend, Kate, had taken to telling me stories and had taught me to bake in the big kitchen at our house and at theirs. We laughed a lot; she always had me repeat the recipes and the story that accompanied it. I laughed at her and told her I didn't have to repeat it because she already knew the story. She always insisted and so I did it, I repeated everything word for word, the recipes, and the story. She would smile and pat my shoulder and tell me I was brilliant. I had loved her like she was my other mother. I had cried along side my best friend when her mother died, it had felt like I also had lost a mother and I spent weeks crying for her. My own mother had cried for her friend and her child, now parentless and moved her into our house as soon as she could. There had been a night that Ava had to stay in a child services home and my mom and dad went to pick her up the next morning after talking to the lawyer. She hadn't spent a night away from us since then. We had spent every night tucked into the stone house where I had been born. Ava was more sister to me than best friend and it was my job to protect her. I looked at Freedom, he had nice black hair, he looked kind of nerdy with his black rimmed glasses perched on his nose. I wondered if he was such a good warlock why he needed them. I had been engrossed in the story he had told, was it true? It matched parts of the professor's story to be true, but was he really telling the truth, was he here to remove or break the curse on Ava? I couldn't get a proper read on him. I would try to keep an open mind and see what he needed from us, but at the first sign of aggression I would end him. He might have gotten away from my first punch, but I knew it wouldn't happen again. I wondered if he knew about the multiple attempts on Ava's life. Had he known the chant would follow her around all her life and involve strangers who tried to hurt her? The questions swirled around my head lightening fast. We had to get home; I noticed the sun had set while we listened to Freedom's tale. My mom had texted and asked what time Ava and I would be home. It was past dinner time now, and I was starting to feel anxious. I always had an uneasy feeling when we left the house or stayed out later than we were supposed to. I knew it was because my parents had placed wards around my house and that was my safe place. I looked at the people seated around the table, Ava, Professor Craig, and Freedom. I felt like these people were the answer to break the curse or chant. To me it was a curse to Freedom it was a chant. Whatever we chose to call it, it would be the downfall of my best friend. Unless we could change it, stop it, finally break it. I decided right there that I needed to find out all I could about the leather book and the chants it held.

Page nine. I needed it. My hand seemed to move toward the book all by itself. As I got closer my fingertips tingled it was a weird sensation. Like little electric shocks went through my hand and wound their way up my arm and into my veins. My jaw clenched as the feeling got stronger. I closed my eyes and imagined water following the ache, the shock, the current of electricity, and slowly my fingers quit tingling then my hand and then my arm. I breathed slowly out of my mouth; my breath hitched as my fingers touched the worn leather book. I have it, I would end this now. My eyes opened and suddenly I was thrown against the back of the chair. It teetered dangerously about to fall and take me down with it. In a whoosh the wooden chair legs squealed, and my chair moved fast toward the wall. The chair back slammed into the wall, my neck snapped sharply as it collided and stopped. I felt like I had a cement weight on my chest, my eyes watered, and I tried to scream but nothing came out. I couldn't breathe, I saw black stars in my vision, oh no, I was going to pass out. I looked up and saw the three of them, their mouths hung open their eyes wide in surprise. Then Freedom stood up and touched the book, closed it up and brought it to his chest in a hug. Like he would cradle a baby, his lips moved silently, like he needed to calm the book down. Slowly the pain in my chest subsided and I gulped in a few deep breaths. My legs started to shake, and I tried to focus on my breathing, slowly I counted each breath and eventually I could breath normally. Freedom still held the book in a bear hug, his eyes were closed, and his lips still moved silently; the professor stood up and started toward me.

I got up out of the chair and yelled, "What the hell was that?!"

My eyes glared daggers at Freedom and darted between him and Ava. Her eyes were huge, and she bit her lower lip. He still hugged the book; his lips moved a bit slower now. His words were still silent to my ears. The professor helped me steady myself. His hand held my elbow gently. He asked if I was all right. I looked into his worried eyes and nodded my head in the affirmative. I gathered my thoughts and looked at Ava once more just to make sure she was ok. Freedom had finally stopped talking to the book and wrapped it in a white cloth and placed it into his backpack. How should I proceed, I knew anger wouldn't work now?

I could hear Ava in my head, *Listen to what he has to say, learn what he needs or wants from us and then proceed with caution.*

I nodded to let her know I heard her. We had just recently developed a telepathic connection. But it was weak, and we had no idea how to control it. The professor brought my chair back to the table, and I hesitantly sat back down. I looked at Freedom, my eyebrow raised up in a silent question. He looked unabashedly at me and smirked.

"The book is charmed. Only my family or my lineage can handle it. It has its own protections. Like I told the professor before, no one has ever touched the book except my family. Now I know why. If you would have asked, I would have told you that. Are you ok? I sometimes let the book know that it has to share what it knows with someone outside of the family and usually it listens." He spoke lovingly of the book like it was a member of his family. I suppose in a way it was. It knew of every member, every chant made and how to ease the suffering of all.

I was unsure how to react to the explanation he gave, I suppose it made sense seeing as how the information inside could harm any number of people. Or get his family in some serious trouble. I heaved a sigh of relief that I was unharmed, my throat was a little sore but all in all I guess I had gotten what I deserved. I had tried to look at the chant book without permission, I had to get my curiosity under control. I knew I couldn't break the curse in one day. My unease at being around Freedom had abated a bit since we had first met. If he had only been a bit more forthcoming with us, this probably wouldn't have happened. The more I thought about it, the more I wondered what Freedom would gain from us breaking the curse. As far as I was concerned there were no selfless people in the world. I would find out his angle. I would figure out his intensions soon enough.

My eyes meet Ava's across the table, and I said, "It's getting late, we should be heading home."

I looked at the professor and then at Freedom, "I'm okay, thank you for telling us your version of the story Freedom." I said. "Ava and I need to discuss the findings with my parents, and with the professor. Are you going to be in town for a while?"

Freedom looked questioningly at the professor and said, "You haven't told them yet?"

Ava and I both turned toward the professor, what news could there be now?

"Ahh girls, I have asked Freedom to stay with me at the guest house until we can figure this thing out. I suppose I thought it would be better to be in close proximity to each other. I spoke earlier to your father, Enid, and he agreed to allow Freedom the opportunity to right his families wrong in this case." the professor said, as he scratched his nose with his wrinkled fingers. "You girls should head on home, and we can talk about this again in the morning."

I stood and picked up my knapsack. Ava followed my lead, she had yet to say anything since I had touched the book and almost fried my brains. The walk to the train station was uneventful, thank goodness. I wasn't sure I could handle any more excitement today. We walked along in silence; I went over the story we had heard tonight and how it compared to the story the professor had told us the other day. There were similarities, it was weird hearing both sides of a story, who, in this circumstance was wrong? On one hand the professor had done what he had, to save Ava's great whatever grandmother's life. It was to ensure that the gypsy, Vano, left them alone and let them live a life together. There was true love there and I knew Ava wouldn't be here on this earth if Vano had succeeded in breaking them apart. Freedom's version of the story was that the Gypsy Vano had been cheated, his family had almost died out because of their greed. Vano had truly loved his family, I had felt all his emotions when I had touched that blasted book. There were truths to both sides. How would we meet in the middle? Both families had suffered terrible losses, and the cycle didn't seem like it could be broken. We had to figure this out. And when we did what would happen to me and my family. We were the protectors of the females in Ava's family, we had been for years. Did we just stop, would our family change because of the chant being broken? I was immersed in my thoughts chasing questions and answers around and around, seeing both sides of the story and their final outcomes. There were a lot. We needed to decide on how to proceed forward. I needed to speak to my parents. I sped up to make sure we didn't miss the train. I turned to speak to Ava and discuss my plans, but I stopped suddenly and looked around. I was completely alone.

CHAPTER NINE

Ava

One minute Enid and I were walking toward the train station and the next it was lights out. I hadn't heard a sound. I tried to open my eyes; it was black like midnight even though I knew we had left the professors house at dusk. We should have been able to get to the end of our train ride before it got pitch black out. Realising then that I did have my eyes open, they were just covered up with a mask or a cloth towel. It smelled like fresh dirt. I tried to breath normal and listen to the surrounding sounds before I started to move. Whoever had taken me, I didn't want them to know I was awake yet. The air I breathed in was hot, not the fresh cool outside air but stale hot air. I was curled up on my side on a hard floor. I felt the motion then, I wasn't on a floor. I was in a moving vehicle. I heard voices in the distance.

Singing. What were they singing? It was a radio. A local station, I think. So, I should still be in Edinburgh. But not local, they spoke a different language. I didn't know it right now because my thoughts were scrambled around. I knew a lot of languages and as I listened, I heard Turkish. Turkish radio station. Where was I? I stretched out and my feet hit a wall. It was rock solid. I tried to move my arms, but they were bound together, I tried to feel how big the space was. I tried to scoot around, and I easily felt the other side of my prison. Ok. Time to take inventory of my situation. I was blind folded, hands tied, small space, probably the trunk of a car. I didn't have anything covering my mouth, but I couldn't speak, my feet were tied together but I could move them around. In my mind I tried to feel Enid, oh no where was she? Had she been taken too? Who knew where we were? Did Freedom have anything to so with this? If so, what had happened to Professor Craig? Would I lose him so soon after learning he was a part of my family? The only person I had that was related to me. The questions mounted and began to pile up on each other, my thoughts raced around. I took a breath and counted to three. Let it out slowly and breathed in again and again I let it out slowly. I needed a cool head right now, I needed to figure out where I was, who had taken me and how I was going to get home again. Focus Ava, I chided myself. Ok, I pictured Enid, her dark curly hair, her eyes, her tiny nose holding her glasses. I knew she had heard me tonight when I had told her to listen to Freedom. Talking to her telepathically was new to us, but I'm glad I had tried. She had nodded her ascent to me. So, I was sure she had heard me. I concentrated on her and tried to sense her, her favorite smell, vanilla, her favorite color, blue. I got nothing. It felt like I was butting my mind against a glass wall. I could picture Enid, but I couldn't get her to hear or talk to me. I tried her mom, Lisa, and her dad, Mitch. Nothing. How was it possible. Finally, I thought to try Professor Craig. I heard him, it was fuzzy though, like having bad cell phone reception.

I yelled in my mind. *Find me, I've been taken.*

I heard Turkish radio. I was exhausted, my head was pounding, my throat was parched. I drifted in and out for what seemed like hours. When the vehicle finally stopped, I heard voices, it sounded like they were arguing I could make out some words but not enough to figure out who they were and what they wanted with me. Finally, I heard a loud click, someone had opened the trunk lid. Hands grabbed me by the shoulders and knees, and I was lifted out of the space. I immediately sensed the difference in the air, it was cool, and I could breathe in deeply. My chest expanded with relief. The mask was lifted off my eyes but before I could see who had captured me, a gloved hand waved in front of my eyes and made everything blurry. I could see the outline of things around me though. I opened my mouth to scream, and nothing came out. I heard my scream in my head, but nothing came out of my mouth. What was happening?

A deep voice close to my ear spoke to me, "You will be ok, we wont harm you. We are here to use the facilities and get a drink of water." It continued to softly whisper to me, "Do not run or try to escape, you will be unable to."

I nodded my head as I realised, I did need to pee and that might give me a few minutes by myself to figure out how to escape. The person guided me, he took my elbow with his warm hand, my feet had been untied, but wait, I hadn't felt any rope. Had my bindings been magical. Was that how my vision was blurred. Was that why I couldn't reach Enid or any of my family? I needed to leave a message somehow. Hopefully, somebody would see or hear me and help my family find me. I was a witch, what could I do, where did I start? I wished that I had that stick of my mothers. Where did that thought come from, I wondered. I heard the bathroom door open, and I was led to a washroom stall. My hands were suddenly loose from their restraints, I tried to push my captor, but I encountered nothing.

A voice in my head spoke quietly to me, *stop trying to escape or it will end badly for you.*

I turned around the bathroom stall and decided to sit and pee… and think, for the minute I had been given. My vision was still blurry. I could hear things though, and I knew there was no one in the bathroom with me so I took my ring off and put it on the toilet lid. Someone would find it.

I felt something on the toilet lid, I grabbed it and held it, it warmed in my hand, it was almost to warm to hold. It felt like a stick. A stick. Hadn't I just wished I had my mother's stick. Was it a wand? I had never thought about it till now. My mother had said the stick was handed down to her through her family. I wish I could remember all the things she had told me about it. All I could remember was that one dream, the one of us running into the forest, the eerie music being played by the white ice cream truck. Someone had tried to steal me, was it a dream? I pushed the thought to the back of my mind, and placed the wand in my back pocket, I needed to figure out how to escape.

Hopefully the ring would be able to communicate to my family where I was. I was pretty sure the ring from Lisa and Mitch was a tracking device, I wondered how come they hadn't found me yet. Then I realised that whoever had taken me probably had cloaked all of me so the best thing to do would be to leave this ring and maybe it would guide them in the right direction and aide them in finding me. I tried a few quick spells, ones to find my vision but they got me nowhere, I still had no idea where I was. I started to get the feeling that I had been in the washroom long enough, I flushed and went to the sink. Thoroughly washed my hands and called out *Halo*.

The door opened softly, and I was escorted back to the waiting vehicle. Quietly I asked if I could ride in the car, I promised I wouldn't try to get out. After a second's hesitation I heard the car door open, and I was placed inside, my seat belt fastened. The bands went around me again, my hands were bound to my lap, my feet felt like they were glued to the floor, my vision was still blurry but this time they didn't put the mask back on me. I listened very quietly to everything. Something to give me an idea of who these people were and why they spoke Turkish, what did they want with me? Did they know I was a witch? They must, I hadn't freaked out when they had blinded me. This had to be connected to Freedom. Why did we ever trust him, his family were the ones who had cursed my family in the first place. They wouldn't want to end it. He must have told his family members where we were and managed to get Enid and I separated somehow.

I hoped the professor was ok. Of course, he would be, one didn't get to be four-hundred years old by being careless. He would know how to find me, he had been monitoring my family, his family, for generations.

As the vehicle drove, miles passed by and I grew sleepy, I shouldn't be tired yet, they must have drugged me or maybe they just put a sleepy spell on me. I smiled, my thoughts were jumbled, I could put a sleepy spell on them too. I wiggled and remembered the stick in my back pocket, how could it help me out of this situation. That was my last thought before I fell into the blackness of sleep.

CHAPTER TEN
Freedom

The room seemed smaller once the two girls had left. I was tired from talking the chant book down. I had never seen it so riled up before, it had been kind of exciting to see the power the book had to protect itself from others.

I waited while the professor gathered up his stuff and locked up his classroom. I would be heading to their house to be a guest in their home. I wonder if my grandfather or mother, Vano or Rose, ever thought that would happen. One of us being welcomed into the home of a cursed one.

It had taken me years to decide on my course of action. I had monitored Ava and Enid since they were about twelve years old. I had kept my distance, shadowed my thoughts and plans, unwilling to let them see me, for fear of discovery. I knew them. I had watched and planned. They were within my grasp; I could feel it. The timing was right, I knew Ava had planned to leave to try and break the chant. She would have been in big trouble. She had no idea what the whole chant contained; she didn't know she was the key. She had no idea of all the people from this world and the other world that were after her. She had no idea her mother and all her female relatives still shielded her. I wasn't sure how long they were going to be able to do that. I knew the chant had weakened as it had every year since it had been cast.

My heart hurt as I felt the anguish my grandfather had felt as he had cast it. I tried not to think of that time long past, but I was tired and weak right now. So, it invaded my soul, I tried to push the feelings out, but it hurt. My heart hurt, like it was being torn in two. I groaned a little and the professor looked up at me.

"Are you all right, Freedom?" he asked as he zippered up his sweater. The nights always seemed cold in Edinburgh.

"Just a little tired professor" I replied with a grin. "It's not everyday you get to meet the object of a four-hundred-year-old chant and then have to talk a chant book down from trying to wreak havoc in a university."

Craig smiled a weary smile at me and gave a little chuckle. Shook his head and said, "I wish sometimes that I hadn't hid myself and Edina from Vano. That we could have helped each other out instead of hurting each other for years. There are not many witches, warlocks or gypsies left on this earth now and I feel we need each other more than ever. I feel the earth shifting as I never have before. Something big is coming Freedom and we will need to stop it together."

We walked out the door, the professor closed and locked it and then put the key in his sweater pocket. My knapsack felt heavy on my back, like the chant book was tired too. As we exited the university I noticed the wind, howling through the trees, like it was crying. The stars had started to twinkle in the sky, that meant no clouds, so again, no rain tonight. Thank goodness, I was always anxious when it rained. I would wonder if that would be the last day we saw.

I began to feel the end of the world was near, the professor was right in thinking the earth had changed, it had, I knew it. Should I share the knowledge with him, no. I couldn't share, it was my burden. I was the one who had to break the chant. And I needed Ava to help me, she was the key. She had to pay the price required and it had to be given freely. I needed to get her alone. I had to try explaining without telling her the whole truth. I needed to get Enid out of the way, but how? They were always together. For years I had watched them grow closer and closer. The only time they were apart was during their classes and those would finish this week. My thoughts rambled around in my head. I always tried to figure out the moves of my grandfather, Vano and my mother, Rose and tried to be one step ahead of them. There was something wrong with them. I thought about my upbringing, they had tried to teach me to hate, to wish bad onto others who had snubbed their noses at us. I rubbed the heart locket in my pocket. A gift. I treasured it. It was from Rose when I was told she was my mother. The lies. I should have thrown the locket away, but I couldn't bring myself to do it. It was an heirloom, the heart had been passed down to Rose from her mother, Vano's wife, my grandmother. I knew at one time I had a family, and they had loved me. I remembered my cousins, now all but gone. They had raised me to love, I knew the stories, I had read the love in the book. The deaths also but that was inevitable. Everyone had to die, didn't they? What had happened to Vano and Rose, did they give a piece of themselves away every time they used the chant to stay young and on this earth. Had they done it to me as well?

The professor and I made our way across the university campus, the wind had picked up and the leaves twirled around our shoes. I swore I heard the howl of the wind, kind of like a shriek. How was it possible that the sky was clear, but it felt like a storm was on its way? The professor talked as we walked, and I listened to half of what he had said. I gave a start when he said another warlock was needed.

I turned to him and asked, "Another warlock? Is that necessary?"

He stopped, touched my elbow and answered, "Time is running out Freedom," he paused "can't you feel the energy? There is good and evil, and I fear evil is winning this war. I am at a loss with what will come next, I am getting old, and I need the help of another. I've found who I need, I just haven't pinpointed his location. But I will continue to work on it."

He turned away and started toward the train station. Suddenly he fell to his knees his breath whooshed out of him. I rushed forward and lay him on his back. What happened to him? His lips turned blue, and his face looked pale white. I checked for a pulse; it was there but it didn't feel very strong. His eyes were closed then suddenly they blinked a couple times, and he moved his head around like he needed to see his surroundings. He turned back to me; he made eye contact and then tried to sit up. I helped him to sit. For just a minute he looked his age for the first time since I had met him.

He said in a shaky voice, "I believe we have a little problem on our hands, I feel my time is coming to an end and Ava is in trouble." He leaned into me for a moment as I helped him stand upright.

"I know Ava is in trouble that is what I am trying to stop, but I need her help and I have to make sure I am able to gather all the ingredients to counter the chant." I replied.

"No Freedom, Ava is in trouble right now." He interrupted me.

His voice seemed surprisingly strong again, the color had returned to his face, and he started walking very fast toward the train station.

"What do you mean, right now?" I tersely asked him "And are you going to tell me what just happened to you?"

"I have had a tracking spell on Ava since she turned ten, it's a generational tracking so I always knew where to find them if I was needed. I never had need of it before tonight. What happened to me was that I felt Ava lose consciousness but not for long. I know she's far away. I am not sure exactly what direction she is headed, and I keep getting interrupted by Turkish music." Professor Craig mumbled the last sentence more to himself than to me.

"So, we are headed to their house now?" I questioned him.

"Yes, I will get a better location on her amongst her personal things." He answered a little out of breath, we had almost run to the train station by this time.

We hadn't left the apartment much later than Ava and Enid had. Only about a half an hour, so she couldn't be to far away could she. We reached the station and purchased our tickets and waited impatiently for the last train.

Then the professors cell phone started ringing.

CHAPTER ELEVEN

Enid

Where did she go? I turned around and called Avas name. There was no reply. Ava wouldn't play a game with me right now. She knew I hated hide and seek and besides we hadn't played that since we were eight years old, and I had lost her in the shopping mall. Our moms had been furious and made us promise to never play that again. I pulled out my phone to call her but all I got was her voicemail. I hung up and put my phone back in my pocket. Then I pulled it out again and dialed my mom. She answered on the first ring.

"Halo" she sounded out of breath.

"Hi mom, its me Enid. Has Ava called you?" I sounded a little breathless, I needed to calm down. "Mom, we were walking to the train, and I guess I got in front of her, she's disappeared, like within a matter of seconds. I tried to call her but all I got was her voice mail. Mom, I'm kind of freakin' out. I didn't mean to lose her. I was thinking about the recipe puzzle and then I tried to hurry so we wouldn't miss the train. I didn't even hear her, or any noise come to think of it. That's weird, isn't it? I didn't hear any noise at all. Right now, I can hear the traffic, the wind in the trees, there were people walking and I could hear them when they laughed. Someone made me deaf mom. Someone wanted Ava and they took her from me. Oh no, what are we going to do?" I practically sobbed into the phone.

"Go right now to the Queen's Hall and wait for me there." My mom told me "Enid be calm, we will figure out what happened to Ava. Your dad and I are only a couple blocks away. Hold on."

The phone went silent as I was just saying goodbye, had my mom just hung up on me? What was going on, I felt like I was in a play, and I was the only one who knew nothing about the story. I ran the few blocks to where my mom told me to go. I could see the stone building from where I was, I looked across the street both ways before I went across.

It was quiet at this time of the day; it would get busier as the night progressed. People loved the Queen's Hall for the music events it held. The building itself was basic, brick and stone, the rounded windows looked out onto Clerk Street. It was an old church built in 1823 that was remade into a music venue, the list of concerts held here would go on for pages.

I glanced anxiously at my watch, a gift from my parents on my eighteenth birthday. Ava had one like mine but we each had our own personalities, and my parents knew that, so our watches reflected those differences. It had been like that growing up with Ava, we were treated like sisters long before her mom had passed away in that tragic boating accident and she had come to live with us. We were born on the same day, we had celebrated every birthday together, almost every Christmas, and holidays were one big, long sleep over. My eyes filled with unshed tears as I wondered where she could be. I couldn't hear her or feel her. I tried to calm down and listen for her voice, nothing. I looked up as I heard a car roaring down the cobbled streets. A black Mercedes was driving fast down the road, its bumper crunched up to the trunk. Looked like a drunk driver.

    I pulled my phone out to call my mom again. They should have been here by now. I dialed and it went straight to voicemail. I heard sirens in the background. Oh, I hoped no one was hurt. Maybe the police were chasing that drunk driver. My thoughts momentarily hoped that they caught the drunk guy. What a senseless thing to do, why endanger others lives. Take a cab or the rail. I looked at my watch again, it's only been five minutes since I last called my mom and dad. My mom had sounded hurried, I thought she would hurry to get here. I tried to call Ava again and again it went straight to her voicemail. Which meant it was turned off. Why? I tried to locate her with her phone tracker, but I got nothing. I wasn't sure who to call. I didn't have the professors phone number; I didn't have Freedoms number. Freedom! this must be his doing. He had found a way to gain our trust and we just let him in. I should have been more aware. I felt it now. This had something to do with Freedom. I knew the professor and him were going to be staying at our guest house, I had to get home. I wondered again where my parents were. I waited for as long as I could then I headed back to the train and waited impatiently for my train and got on. I didn't know where my parents were or Ava, but I knew the professor and Freedom were headed to my house. I went over our conversation in my head while the train sped me home.

The train ride went quick, the walk to Wester Coates Gardens was uneventful. I walked up my drive and up the stairs in record time. The front porch light was on, but the lights inside were off.

"Mom, Dad" I called out their names hoping for an answer but instead I was greeted by only silence.

I went out back and toward the garden house. The lights were on, and I heard voices. I wretched open the door and four sets of eyes turned towards me. My mom and dad, Professor Craig, and Freedom. They stopped talking midsentence.

"Ava's been taken." The tears, that had been hovering, trailed down my cheeks as I looked at them all. "We were walking and then she just disappeared." I choked out.

My mom and dad each walked toward me and hugged me on either side. My head hung down and I gratefully accepted their hugs. I noticed a set of worn black shoes come stand in front of me. The professor.

I looked up at him and asked, "Why did you let him into our lives? He's a liar and he wants to hurt Ava." I took a gulp of air and continued, "He took her, or he knows who did. This is only happening because he showed up and tried to lure us in with that chant book." I looked over to Freedom; my red eyes shot daggers in his direction.

"Why didn't you answer your phone mom?" I looked up at her and finally noticed the bruises on her cheeks, the cut lip and dirt on her clothing. I let out a small gasp and looked at my father. He had torn jeans, and a black eye was forming as I looked at him. His knuckles were red with blood. Was it his or someone else's? What had happened to them?

"What happened to you guys?" I fairly screamed at them "Are you okay?"

My mom helped me to the kitchen table and gently sat me down across from Freedom, who I noticed hadn't said a word since I came in. I glared again at him my brows furrowed in thought. Why was he still here? My parents should have gotten rid of him by now.

"Enid, honey, we know where Ava is and who took her. It wasn't Freedom. But he does know who did it and we are glad he was here to help us out." My mom stopped to look at Freedom and continued, "It was Freedom's mother, Rose, he said she is not all together there and is out to harm Ava and all of us. We will get her back and fix this don't worry. She should be wearing her watch, or her ring, we have tracking spells on them, as well as on yours. Professor Craig also had a tracking spell on her and will get to work on that aspect right away. I am sorry we didn't answer your phone calls. Both our phones got broken tonight as we had a little run in with a black Mercedes. It smacked us from behind and ran us into the side rails. When we stopped and got out of the vehicle there were two dark haired men who came at us. I suppose they were trying to get us to stop looking for Ava. They warned us not to try looking for her and that you would be next if we didn't listen to them. They smashed the phones and threw them into the hill side. We didn't even try to look for them. The car was damaged beyond repair. We tried to get away, but as you can see, they had a bit more brute strength than us. I thought they were looking for a signal or sign to let us go because after about twenty minutes they just jumped back into their smashed car and drove away. It wasn't to long after that that the police came by and asked if we needed help. We borrowed a phone and called Professor Craig and then tried to call you, but we couldn't get through. Once the police realised, we were going to be ok they hurried after the Mercedes. Craig got our keys and truck from the garage, then he and

Freedom drove out to pick us up. We drove by the Queens Hall, but we didn't see you. We only just gathered in Craigs new home when you arrived." Her hand gently smoothed down my hair and she let her hand rest on my shoulder.

I gulped and took in her story; she hadn't told me the most important part. Where was Ava. She said Freedom knew who had taken her and where she had been taken so I looked up at him across the table from me and very quietly said, "Where is she Freedom, you tell me right now."

He looked me in the eyes and without flinching told me she was unharmed, but he didn't know for how long. He said there was more to the story than he previously told us. So, we gathered some tea and sat around the table while we listened to the rest of the story. I was antsy and thought we should be looking for Ava, calling the police, torturing Freedom. But instead, I held my tongue and waited for the story. Praying that Ava would be unharmed while we sorted this out.

CHAPTER TWELVE

Ava

I couldn't see where we were. I guessed that we had driven for about a half hour. I started getting crampy in my hands and legs, where the invisible bindings circled my ankles and wrists. It had to be getting close to midnight, although my sight was blurry due to the spell, I could see that it was dark out. It had felt like hours since Enid and I had left Professor Craig's house. I wondered how she was, where she was. She must be frantic at my kidnapping; I wished I could talk to her. I had tried multiple times telepathically to get through to her. But something was blocking me. I did get through to the professor, but I was not sure he could understand me, it was more of a feeling I had sent to him, I think. I recalled that the professor had told us he had been keeping tabs on

Enid and me for years. I hoped leaving my ring would send them in the right direction. I hoped a stranger didn't happen upon the ring and take it.

The ride was long, I couldn't eavesdrop, couldn't see, couldn't smell, or talk. Whoever had me, had muffled all my senses. A powerful witch or wizard. Or Gypsy! Was this Freedom's doing. Had we all fallen for his charms and believed his story of wanting to break the chant? His family had placed a chant on my family what more could they want? Why come for me now? A myriad of questions kept popping into my mind. Solutions are what I needed right now, not more questions.

The car started to slow down. My heart rate accelerated. Now might be my only chance to run. The car stopped and I felt someone grab my elbow to guide me out of the car. I scooted out, hoping they would let the spell finally fall away. A voice beside my ear whispered for me to follow them. My feet started to move on their own will. It felt like I had no control over my body.

We walked up five steps and through a door, then it felt like a lot of stairs going upward. I stopped counting at twenty-two. Could we be at a lighthouse? I still couldn't hear, smell, or see. It was beyond frustrating. Finally, we stopped, I gulped in a deep breath, I would need to up my cardio when I got out of this mess. The hand that held my elbow guided me forward again, toward what, I wasn't too sure. I tried to ask them what they wanted but my words sounded like garbled foreign mumbo jumbo. I felt the sweat cool on my back, my arm hair raised up with little goosebumps on my arms, the windows must be opened or else there was air conditioning turned up in here. The floor was solid not bouncy like a rug would be. Finally, we stopped, and I was seated in a chair, I felt the back against my back, it was soft, cushiony. My arms were placed on the arm rests, they were soft too. I heard a voice. It told me that they were going to put a needle in my hand but that it wouldn't hurt. What on earth were they going to put in me? I tried to tell them no; I didn't want a needle. But my voice wouldn't work. I shook my head no, but it was to late. I felt the cool needle as it slipped into my skin, the pinch almost unnoticeable. It was jabbed into the back of my right hand, I felt a piece of tape go over the needle, they were going to leave the needle in me. There was no movement for a brief minute and then I heard the door close softly.

The spell broke as the door closed and I could see, hear, and speak freely. My arms and legs were still bound though, by invisible threads to the soft chair. I turned my head to see if anyone was in the room with me, but I was alone. I looked at the needle in my hand and realised they hadn't put anything in me at all, it was a needle taking my blood out of my hand. I watched transfixed as the red liquid flowed out of my hand through the clear plastic tubing and into a glass vial. The vial slowly moved up and down like a teeter totter. I shook my head, I needed to figure out where I was.

I called out, "Halo? Is anybody there? Where am I and what do you want with me?" there was no answer.

I struggled against the invisible bands that held me in place. I turned my head to look around the room I was captured in. It was elegant to say the least. The furniture was turn of the century, heavy brocade drapes on the wide windows their silky material pooled on the polished wood floors below them. There were bars on the outside of the windows. The sun shone through the windows; it made the golden thread glisten on the drapes. There was a floral design on the wallpaper. A wooden writing table complete with rolltop cover and a dainty chair. The large wooden headboard was golden with a leafy design, maybe painted, with a puffy silky fabric held together with large buttons. The bedding was silk and shiny. There were two side tables each held a little reading lamp. My trainers were still intact and clean, which meant there was no mud. I listened for traffic. Nothing. I did hear the whistle of birds though.

It had to be close to twelve hours since I had been taken. Unless, I had been asleep for more than a couple hours. The silence started to get to me. I wondered how long I would have the needle stuck in me, draining my blood. Would it be until I died? A very slow painful death that would be. I gave a little shudder as I thought of that. Someone had to come change the vial sooner or later, right?

I was all alone, and I wasn't sure my new telepathic abilities worked very well. I had tried multiple times to send messages to Enid, Lisa, Mitch, and Professor Craig since I had woken up. I missed the sound of the traffic. I didn't spend a lot of time in the country.

Finally, I heard the whisper of shoes on the wooden floor. The steps were light and quick like someone was walking very fast toward me. I looked at the doorway and wondered who was going to come face to face with me. I held my breath and counted to three then slowly let it out. I would need all my wits about me if I was going to figure out what all this meant. The person stopped outside my door, and I heard a key slide into the lock, it turned slowly then opened, the handle turned, and the heavy wooden door silently slid open. A tiny little woman stood there and looked at me.

Her dark hair was chopped short, her eyes a piercing grey she looked to be about my age maybe a bit older. She had on a suit of the darkest blue, almost black. The cut and fit looked fabulous on her. She looked vaguely familiar. Where had I seen her? She looked behind her and shut the door quietly.

"Halo Ava" she said in a musical voice, "My name is Majestic, I am a friend of Professor Craigs. I am here to help you get out of this mess."

"Where am I? And what do these people want with me?" I questioned her.

"Let's get you out of here first, then I will try to answer all your questions, okay?"

"Okay, but how can you undo my bonds? I'm stuck to this chair with invisible rope. It feels like metal bands are holding my wrists and ankles together. Whoever took me is powerful, I have been blinded, and they took away my sense of smell and my hearing. And last of all I have this needle in my hand, can you get it out of me and keep my vial of blood, I don't want anybody walking around with my DNA except me."

The lady, Majestic, calmly walked over to me and placed her hand on my wrist and closed her eyes. I heard her mutter something under her breath but couldn't make out the words. Suddenly my wrists and ankles were free. I stood up and rubbed at my wrists and took the tape, which held the needle in my hand, off.

Majestic grabbed my hand and gently said, "Here let me help you with this." She quickly pulled the needle out of my hand. It stung a little and she looked at me and asked if I was ok to walk and run if needed. She got to her feet; she really was tiny; her head only went to my shoulders.

She looked at me like she had to make sure I was all there and said, "Its nice to finally meet you."

"What do you mean, finally?" I asked her as I pushed a stopper in the vial holding my blood and put it in my jacket pocket.

Smiling, she replied, "Later, I will tell you everything later."

Listening closely, she walked to the door, and opened it slowly. She poked her head outside and motioned me closer to her. I hurried forward and she grasped my hands.

Majestic looked back at me, "we are going to walk very fast and be as quiet as we can, the kidnappers are outside in the garage. There are three floors, we need to get to the bottom and out the front door. My car is parked at the edge of the long driveway. There are clusters of trees outside, we need to run from tree to tree and avoid detection. I have muffled our steps, but they will hear us if they are listening for any noise."

I nodded my head in understanding. Together we silently slipped through the door, and I closed it softly behind me. We walked as quietly as we could on the polished wooden floor. The stairs were a little more complicated and I cringed as I heard a loud creak when I stepped on one. There were only two more floors to go, I was almost free. A toilet flushed on the floor below us and suddenly a door opened, we stopped and held our breath. Majestic quietly peered over the railing and watched as a tall man walked down the hallway and then we heard another door open and close. She looked back and motioned me forward. Quickly and quietly, we continued our descent. After what seemed like forever, we reached the front door. Majestic turned the front door handle and opened it, just as the back door opened too. We looked behind us down the long hallway and saw a woman and a tall man come into the house. They looked at us in stunned silence for half a second before they raised their hands.

Majestic grabbed my hand and pulled me out the front door

and then we were running for our lives. Across the green grass we darted from tree to tree. As we ran, I smelled burning and looked back to see the trees behind us burning. They had shot fireballs from their hands! We were just yards from the end of the driveway, and I knew Majestic's car would be there waiting for us. At the last tree we stopped for a moment. I looked at Majestic and saw her grey eyes were burning bright like purple verbena. She muttered something again under her breath; we heard a scream and then we ran again. We zigzagged to avoid the bolts of fire that were shot at us. We were almost to the end of the drive when I heard Majestic scream. A bolt of fire had hit her in the arm and bounced off, it lay smoldering on the wet grass; it made a hissing sound as it fizzled out. She stumbled but didn't fall. I grabbed her arm and got her to run again. The car was there, black, the doors were flung open, and we jumped in. We accelerated so fast I was thrown against the back seat; I looked up, I saw a fire ball hurtling toward us and screamed. Majestic looked up, raised her hand, and waved her fingers. The fireball disappeared. As we drove away, I saw the lady scream at us and then turn away, probably to look after the tall man. Majestic must have hit him with whatever she had mumbled as we were running away.

I glanced up and saw who was driving the car. It was a beautiful younger guy, his bright shock of red hair so typical of the men in this area, then his eyes met mine in the rear-view mirror and I let out a soft gasp, his eyes were like looking into the greenest pasture when the sun glinted off the rocky hillside. I was momentarily stunned by his gaze. I'm sure I hadn't met him before. Beside him sat Enid, she looked at me calmly, but I could see the tears in her eyes. I reached for her hand, and she reached for mine at the same time, we were crying and babbling together incoherently.

"I am so sorry I lost you, are you ok, are you hurt, I'm sorry, it will never happen again." Enid said between big gulps of air.

"I'm ok, everything will be ok, I'm hungry." We let go of each others' hands and looked at each other, Enid's face was streaked with tears. She looked like she hadn't slept in days. "I'm ok." I repeated to her.

She nodded her head and looked over at Majestic, gasped and said, "Are you ok Majestic?"

I turned my head and looked at the person who had just saved me from a kidnapping and then from fireballs being hurled at us. She had a shimmer of sweat on her face and her eyes were glossy.

"Oh Majestic, how can I help you?" I asked her, as her eyes rolled up in her head, she moaned a little before she slumped down in her seat, losing consciousness. I took her wrist and felt for a pulse. There was one but it was faint.

I looked at Enid and said, "We need to help her, and who is driving?"

"Ava, this is Ian, my boyfriend. And Majestic is the twin sister to Majic, the warlock, who helped bring us together with the protection spell so many generations ago." She briefly took her eyes from mine and looked to Ian; worry reflected in her gaze. He looked at me in the rear-view mirror and nodded and took one hand off the steering wheel to run his hand gently over Enid's shoulder.

"Nice to meet you, Ava." His deep voice was the perfect pitch of baritone, "Not quite the meeting I had in mind when Enid told me I was finally going to meet her family and best friend. We are headed back to Professor Craig; he will be able to help Majestic if we get her to him in time." His gaze darted to Majestic who lay still beside me, her breathing was laboured and weak.

I looked up with surprise to Enid's eyes. How did he know about magic, witches, and warlocks? He seemed strangely at ease for someone who had just outrun fireballs. Enid passed me a folded-up jacket to put under Majestic's head and told me we would have a conversation once we were safely back home and around the kitchen table. I felt the weight of the past twenty-four hours descend on me and I lay my head back against my seat, put my seatbelt on and drifted off in an exhausted slumber. When I awoke, we were headed down the street toward our house. I could see the lights were on and Lisa and Mitch came out to the road to watch as we arrived. The car stopped in the driveway and Mitch opened the door to grab Majestic while Lisa opened my door and practically yanked me out to give me a tight hug.

She held me at arms length and looked at me. "Are you really ok Ava?"

"I will be fine, I need a shower, a change of clothes and some food. Then we need to figure out who is trying to hurt me and what they want. But first, a shower."

I gave her a small smile, a quick hug and walked up the steps to the open door. Professor Craig was there he watched and waited. I glanced at him but offered no conversation. I started up to my room and I heard Mitch bring Majestic inside. The professor told him to bring her to the couch and that's all I heard. I closed my bedroom door and headed to my bathroom to strip. The vial of blood fell from my jacket, it lay innocently on the rug glaringly red against my clean carpet. I picked it up and placed it on the counter to deal with later. Something poked my back and I reached into the back pocket of my jeans and there split in half was my mother's wand, I cried then. I didn't have many things of hers left and I had connected with this part of her. I still didn't know how it appeared to me when I had wished for it. I left my clothing in a heap by the door and stepped into the hot shower, it was exactly what I needed, the hot pelting water started to heat up my ice filled veins and then I started to shake. Tears poured down my face. I sat under the water, unable to stand a moment longer and wept. Why had this happened to me. Was it because of the Professor and his wife? I was so angry.

My tears blended with the water, and I watched as they twirled down the drain disappearing until I had cried all I could. I must get to the bottom of this. I wont be taken again. I thought back to the conversation I had overheard in the car. Were there any clues for me there? All I could remember was that everything had been muffled. They had given me no clues. The water started to cool off, I stood up and rinsed the soap off, washed my tear-stained face and turned the faucet off. I grabbed a warm towel from the warming rack and dried off. I was shaken but otherwise unharmed. I needed to acknowledge the silver lining in my abduction. I wrapped a towel around my hair and dressed in sweatpants and a well worn soft blue t-shirt. I slipped my feet into my slippers and hung up my towels. Grabbed my brush and ran it tiredly through my damp hair. Then I gave my teeth a good brushing. I felt a bit better and then I heard my stomach grumble. I took a deep breath and headed out of my room ready to get back downstairs. I needed to see how Majestic was doing and I needed food. Then I remembered Ian, the boyfriend, how did he fit into all this mess? I really needed to talk with Enid. The vial of my blood lay innocently on the bathroom counter completely forgotten.

CHAPTER THIRTEEN

Ian

I suppose it was fitting that I was here in this house with a vial of Ava's blood laying about carelessly upstairs. She had no idea how important her blood was. Would now finally be the time to tell them all? I saw the worry on Enid's face. I had come to really care for her over the past two years. I wondered if they needed to know everything, after all, we had rescued Ava with out too much damage. She told us she hadn't left any of her blood at the mansion so that part would be safe. I had helped the professor heal Majestic as best we could. I can't intervene to much, there are rules to follow after all. The burns on Majestics side and arm are extensive and I am glad they hadn't hit her square on. She would need to rest and heal before doing any more magic or she would risk burn out. I noticed how her eyes had gone flat when the fireball had hit her. Before she passed out, I saw the ring of black around the brilliant grey of her irises. It worried me then and it still did. I knew she would be fine, but I couldn't reveal my knowledge just yet. I listened for sounds coming from the stairs to see if Enid had come back down. She had excused herself as soon as she could. She needed to get cleaned up a bit before Ava came back down. I had mixed a calming herbal tea and waited for her at the kitchen table. Lisa, Mitch, and Freedom were there and talked quietly they looked up at me as I set the teacup down softly on the table.

"How is Majestic doing?" Mitch asked me.

Lisa looked up and stirred some honey into her cup as she waited for my answer. Freedom looked uncomfortable and just sat with his hands stuffed into his pockets, his dark hooded eyes looked at me with unasked questions. I got the feeling he knew a bit more about me than he had let on.

"She's resting as comfortably as we could make her, I'm worried about the hit she took though. Rest will be the best thing for her now. I can stay on the floor beside her tonight and the professor will take a turn early in the morning so I can catch a few moments of sleep. We have done everything we know to do; we have to just wait and hope her fever breaks through the night." I reached over to grab a scone, Lisa must have baked them up recently, it was warm and melted in my mouth. "I'm glad I was able to help you with this tonight. I suppose you would like to know more about me and how I know about all this stuff, especially all the stuff about your families."

Mitch smiled a small smile, "Yes, answers are needed but let's wait until we all can sit together, then we would like to hear your part in this tale."

"Ok, we will wait a bit. Lisa these are delicious, thank you for baking them up." She gave me a small smile and a quick nod of her head in acknowledgement. I finished the scone and debated weather to grab another when Enid entered the kitchen, she looked refreshed in clean jeans and a dark blue sweater. She had washed her face and combed her hair. Her lips glistened with a pink gloss. She was beautiful. I wondered briefly at our future together; would it happen? I wouldn't look, I guessed we should leave that part up to fate. If the world could be saved, I figured we could have a shot at a long relationship.

As usual though, the world came first, as it had my whole life. She smiled at me as I passed her the warm tea, she sipped and closed her eyes. Then she took the chair beside mine and curled her one leg under her and sat down. She rested her head on my shoulder for a moment before she settled down in her chair and continued to drink her tea. My heart squeezed it was so full of love, more than I had thought possible. I hoped she loved me back. I hoped she could forgive me. I hope she would see that what I do is for the world, for mankind, and I mean to take care of that before I tell her that I love her.

I heard footsteps coming down the carpeted stairs and within a moment, Ava entered the room. She looked better, although I could tell she had been crying. Her eyes were red rimmed and puffy, but she was clean, and her hair was brushed. There was a skin-colored bandage on the back of her hand where the needle had punctured her delicate skin. How much should I tell them? Always aware that what I knew could change the course of the actions everyone had to take. It literally could mean the end of this world. She looked at everyone seated around the table and sat down at the head in the captain's chair. I passed her the fresh scones; she took one and broke a few little pieces off to eat. The professor came back into the kitchen and looked at all of us. He sat in a chair at the opposite end of Ava, the far end of the table. Enclosed in this homey kitchen I wondered at all the lives that we all hold close to us. Our families, brothers, sisters, aunts, uncles, nieces, nephews, mothers, and fathers. Where did we draw the line, what life becomes more important than our own?

The seven of us, eight if I counted Majestic, must agree on the actions that we take from here on out. I moved silently out of my chair and stood up; every eye turned to me. They waited expectantly to hear what I had to say, so I started.

"It was really nice to finally meet all of you, unfortunately it wasn't under the best circumstances. I met Enid two years ago, online. It was orchestrated." Enid looked at me with a question in her eyes and opened her mouth to talk but I keep on going.

"Our meeting was supposed to be as friends, so I could help her, help Ava. I knew about Ava trying to break the curse, I knew about the curse long ago. I knew most of Ava's ancestors and Craig's as well." I gulped in a breath and looked at them all one at a time.

This was going to be a bit harder than I had thought it would. It had been so long since I had belonged to humans, roamed among them freely. They all had questions; I could see it in their eyes. I needed to tell them more.

My heartbeat clamored along loudly in my chest, but I continued, "I know you all have questions you are just wanting to shout out to me but let me finish my side of the story and then I will answer everything I am able to." I waited till they all had nodded their heads in agreement.

"My family is from a long line of warlocks and witches, so long ago even I can't remember the beginning of our family. We are much more than that though. Some people would call us gate keepers, divine beings, or even gods. My family made sure the world was kept in balance, we helped even out the hatred and the love. Every once in awhile we got to stay earth bound to make sure the balance was kept. I have had many brothers and sisters throughout time, we are like the stars in the sky. We burn brightly and sometimes we just die off. I have a brother; he keeps to himself. He is on earth with me now. Just the two of us. His name is Tyler. He told me about the grumblings of a curse brought on by love and how it would affect the whole world one day. We are not able to control free will, but we can give multiple choices. The person who chooses their role in our universe does so at their own choice. It's hard to explain my family role and how it intersects with all of yours. But know that we are on your side Ava, we need you to figure out your family history, change the course of the curse or our world, your world, will be affected drastically. I am not able to tell you how, as the choices you make must be your own. I am only here for guidance; I need to make sure the choices you all make do not swing the balance of good or evil to heavily. I was meant to only be on the peripheral of your world, but I met Enid, and I knew it was my turn to be on this earth, so here we are, together tonight to decide the fate of the world. Who has the first question?"

I took my seat next to Enid; she jumped up and walked away. My heart broke a little at her rejection. I supposed I shouldn't have expected anything else. I had been keeping myself from her for the last two years. Which to me is a blink of an eye, my life was eternal or so I thought. I looked at the others. Waited. It didn't take long before the questions began.

"How could you know and not fix or break the curse before it began?" Ava's question stood out from the rest, so I turned to her and addressed her first.

"According to the line of life eternal, your family had to be cursed. I am unable to tell you why or how to break it. That is up to you and your friends, we were able to make sure you had the opportunities to gather the information you needed to counter the chant. Come on Ava, is there a more pressing concern you should address?" I urged her to think of a more important question. I watched as her brows furrowed together in thought. I looked up as Freedom questioned me next.

"Your family is able to sit and watch as our lives unfold, yet you say the balance is always kept. There are wars, famine, crime, and injustices all over the world. And you just let it happen? My ancestors put a four-hundred-year chant on a family, which meant it would harm or cripple the descendants of Craig and Edina. These people would suffer their whole lives, they wouldn't even know of Craig or Edina except as the reason there was a chant to begin with. Were they just pawns to you? Lives to play chess with. What are you here for now? You have had the ability to stop or intervene for years, so why now? The chant is almost at its completion. There's more and you aren't telling us what it is. What made you come to earth, stay, and intervene now? That's my question." Freedom leaned back in his chair and folded his hands on his stomach.

He looked the picture of relaxation, but I knew underneath his pose, he was trembling.

"Yes Freedom, my family and I have always been here guiding mankind through terrible famine, droughts, wars and plagues. It is not our choice to promote peace love and happiness, we are here to ensure that with all the terrible traumas come the positive outcomes afterwards. Without evil there cannot be harmony, it is what rips us apart that makes us stronger as one." I took a brief pause to look into his eyes, "The chant your family made was one of desperation, hatred and of sadness. Your family has always felt all emotions deeply, more so than any family we have encountered over many years. I understand your question, why now. Well, the chant is almost complete, there is more but I am unable to tell you what. Its up to all of you to figure out your next steps."

I looked around the table once more and meet the eyes that were riveted on me. I felt the questions which burned in their faces, in my peripheral vision I saw movement. Enid. She hadn't said anything for the last half hour. My heart squeezed, what would her decision be, did she love me enough? With all my knowledge and talent, this one beautiful, birdlike human could hurt me like no other. My heart was in her hands. She looked at me for a full minute and then looked at all the people gathered around the kitchen table. There was a war going on in her mind. I knew she felt she must protect Ava, its part of what made up her DNA, but her heart was human, and I knew it was breaking a little, I could feel it. She would choose them and save Ava rather than choose me. My heart crushed; I felt pain like I had never felt in all my years. I hurt because I had been the one to make her choose and that hurt her. I cannot cry, that emotion would hurry the end of the world along. I watched her and saw the beginning of tears gathered in the corners of her eyes. The way her back straightened; her shoulders sat back; her head held high. The swallow she took before she looked into my eyes. Her mouth quivered a little before she breathed. My heart split open; red poured throughout my body leaving little puddles everywhere.

"Thank you for the information you have given us Ian and thank you for helping us find Ava tonight. Right now, according to your own words, you cannot help us anymore." A tear fell from one eye, and she hastily swiped at it with the back of her sweater. "You have given us enough information that we know we have to figure out how to stop the chant from completion but that we have to do it on our own. I think that you should leave now so we can start to figure it out. Goodbye Ian."

She walked out of the kitchen, I heard her sob, and it broke me. She had asked me to leave. I cannot stay now. She had made her choice. I stood up and wished Ava and the rest of the group good luck and let them know they could do this they didn't need my help at all. I walked through the dark house to the front door. It was a nice house, full of pictures and memories and warmth. They would be able to finish this, they were a strong group. I grasped the door handle and turned to take one last look behind me. They would be ok; Enid would be too. But would I? I closed the door softly behind me and took a step down the stairs. That's when I saw her, waiting for me. I clenched my hands in a fist and breathed, let my fists slowly unfurl and met her on the grass beside the walkway.

"Is this goodbye, Enid?" I asked her quietly.

"I don't know who you are." she replied in a shaky voice. "You have lied to me for two years; how can I forgive you? Then behave like you are the same person. The person who brought me flowers, who called me late at night to talk, who made me laugh with all the tales of your employee shenanigans. Is your family even real? Or were they a story line in your universe? Am I? I need time to figure out who we are together, am I better off alone and doing my part in the big scheme of the universe. Am I only here to support Ava and her family through this chant? What will happen to me then? You probably already know the answer to these questions, but you won't share them with me. What do we have, it's nothing isn't it? I'm just a pawn in your universal games. I thought you loved me, it's a feeling I got from you. I know we never said it out loud to each other, but I felt it." She wiped the tears which flowed down her porcelain cheeks, her sweater left a red mark on her skin where it rubbed. "You need to leave, and I need to help Ava, she isn't out of danger yet."

Enid stepped out on to the sidewalk and headed back up the stairs before I could mutter up the words and quietly, I said, "Goodbye Enid, I will see you soon. Creator help you on your quest. I love you; I have always loved you."

I'm not sure, but I thought I heard, "I loved you." whispered back.

CHAPTER FOURTEEN
Rose

Oh no, the girl was gone. How would I explain it to Vano, my father. He would likely thrash me, or worse, put a chant on me. We had her and that nasty Majestic got her back. Majestic had been the bane of my existence; she had always popped in just in time to wreck my plans. My father went googly eyed at her and had been trying to woo her for years. He had no idea the trouble she presented to us. I looked down at my feet the tall man was still. I bent over to drag him back inside the mansion. My hair kept falling into my face. He was a lot heavier than I thought he would be. Grunting a little I pulled him a scant foot before I stood up and closed my eyes. I needed to clear my head. My hand fumbled in my jacket pocket and found the smooth rock, my fingers rubbed the stone as I chanted a small incantation under my breath. Slowly

I felt the earth respond to my wish, I turned and slowly walked up the stairs, I felt the tall man, Paul, drift in behind me. I liked being a wizard, my father knew I was special. I had been ever since the day I was born. The day my mother travelled the stars. I remembered everything about my mother, the feel of her wrapped around me as I lay snuggly in her womb. The strong beating of her heart as she breathed life into me. Her warm hands as she cradled me, the sway of her body as she walked and danced. Her voice as she told me stories. I think she knew I would be special even before I was born. The amulet she had given to me before she left us. I thought she had been an angel sent from above to guide our family. The man, Craig and his brassy haired wife, Edina had taken her from all of us before I could learn everything from her. I remembered how I had stayed close to my father in all the years after she had been taken from us. He told me all his stories, the history of the gypsy family, I had memorized the chant book. The birth dates, the deaths, the chants, and their conclusions. The one chant that we had to preserve, the lengths my father had went thru to ensure it would reach its conclusion. The reason why we had to see it through. No one knew. We couldn't ever tell them the truth, let them believe the worst of us, it was preferable to the havoc that would be let loose if the chant was broken.

I stopped in the large living room and rested Paul on the brown chintz couch. He groaned as he was placed down. His eyes opened slowly in confusion. His mouth opened as if to ask me a question, but no words would come out. His eyes grew round as he realized he couldn't speak, I rested my hand on his arm and said,

"Easy Paul, you will be ok, the hit you took from Majestic was a hindering spell. It will wear off in a little while. For now, just lie still and concentrate on your breathing. I cant change anything for you, we have to just wait."

I waited until I noticed the change in his eyes, the waiting had begun.

CHAPTER FIFTEEN
Professor Craig

There were five of us who sat around the table that Ian and Enid had just left. Majestic was sleeping fitfully, the potion I had given to her to heal had left her resting. That left me to act as the head of the group. I was the oldest after all, and the reason the chant had been cast in the first place. I could see the new information that Ian had given us was a shock to everyone. I had an inkling that there was a higher power to our universe, and I think we just met him. Or a part of his family anyways. I would have to ask Enid some pointed questions when she returned. Lisa and Mitch are in a quiet conversation, discussing their roles in the universe no doubt. Ava is asking questions to Freedom, something about a recipe. I heard the front door whisper close and a moment later Enid was back with us. Her eyes were red rimmed, and her cheeks were blotchy. She had been crying and I felt for her, the universe was a tricky road to follow. She put her glasses back on and sat down quietly in her chair. Then she rose again and investigated the empty chair that Ian had just vacated. Going to the sink she filled the tea kettle with water and put it on the stove to heat up. I would wait a few minutes to ask those important questions of her. I cleared my throat, and everyone looked up at me.

"I know we have had quite a surprise and now we have a lot to process but I think the most pressing matter now is to figure out who took Ava and what they wanted from her. The curse needs to be figured out too."

Enid looked up at me and almost yelled, "You think? You actually think that is the most pressing question? We have just learned that we are pawns in a game of the universe, and you need to know who kidnapped Ava?!" she stopped and took in a shaky breath before she calmly continued, "I'm sorry Professor Craig and Ava, I am just thinking about the roles we have played, and I wonder why? Why did this happen to us? What made us so special that we became the main pieces in the big puzzle of the universe? Why did a god decide we were worthy of him taking part in our lives? He became a mortal to be with us, with me, to guide us all and I wonder why?"

"I know you have had a shock, we all have Enid, but before we begin to question all the games of the universe, we still have the problem that started this all. We need to break the chant; Ian told us that much. We need to know why Ava was taken and basically unharmed. She must be the key to the problem, now we have to figure out how she fits. I know you and Lisa have figured out a problem within the recipe book that Katherine left for you. Would you share what you have found with us?"

Enid looked quickly at her mother and then reached into her

pocket and brought out a folded piece of paper, she walked to the table and tried to flatten it out, but the creases prevented it from laying flat. She turned her back and removed the whistling teapot and turned the burner off. I looked at the paper and turned it right side up, it was in the form of a recipe, is this what Ava and Freedom had been whispering about. Lisa rose and took another paper from her pocket and placed it unfolded on the table beside her daughters. I put them side by side to see what they had found. It looked like a recipe for baking…

New

Stir

½ cup

Scots Pine needles

Lavender

1 tsp vanilla

Essence of Amorphophallus Titanum (corpse flower)

Rhododendrons (pink pearl) seeds

Cherry leaves

Wych Elm leaves in July

Mix gently ten times clockwise

Add crushed yew berries

Ichor mixed gently

The list was extensive it was as long as the paper it was written on. I wondered out loud how it had been completed.

Lisa answered me this time, "Enid had been given a cookbook from Katherine, and every year on her birthday I gave her an envelope which contained a recipe and a story. Katherine didn't tell me what it was for, only that I needed to give the envelopes to Enid on her birthday, we were to read the story and then make the recipe. When we were done baking, we were to place the letter in the cookbook. Not long ago the book needed to be looked at and Enid saw the words highlighted and began to write them down, however they didn't make any sense to her and so she called me and asked me to look in the book and confirm the letters and words that had been highlighted. Enid thought we could work together to figure out what it meant, however, when I looked at the book, the highlighted words and letters were all different than the ones Enid had been shown. Together little by little we pieced the words together and realised it was a recipe, we thought it must be a message from Katherine. I have been looking for places to purchase some of the ingredients, but I cannot figure out how we are to get the essence of the corpse flower. It only blooms once every so often, I was not even sure when that would happen." She let out a breath and looked at Enid, but Mitch was the one who answered her.

"The corpse flower, Amorphophallus Titanum more commonly known as Titan Arum, blooms once every couple of years in 2015, 2017, and in 2019 where for the first-time people had seen and recorded it. It blooms at night and the strongest smell is during the first few hours, it really smells like cheese, but some people say it smells like rotting flesh. If we need that essence, I can get us in the night opening. The flower is closely guarded and is on the endangered plant list I am not sure we could get close to it. I will see what the plans are for the public entrance. It should be happening soon as the flower blooms around the end of June for about a week."

We all looked at him as he finished his sentence. "Well, that would be very helpful. Thank you, Mitch." I filled in the silence by giving a little cough into my hanky.

"I think we need to figure out the recipe, when will we be able to have all the ingredients to try it out?" I asked the room at large.

Mitch answered me first, "I think most of the ingredients can be bought or picked around the end of June, the only thing we need here that can only be obtained once is the corpse flower essence so; once we have the essence of that we should be able to complete the recipe. Until then we should be vigilant of each other, Lisa and I will get some new cell phones, the professor, Lisa, and I should tighten the security around the house and on Ava and Enid. Freedom, we will need you to keep an eye on your mom and grandfather if you see them or any of your other family members who seem out to harm Ava in any way. Professor, you, and Freedom can stay here in our house in the guest rooms and help keep an eye on Majestic, I have a feeling we will need her help when we complete the recipe. The girls still have a final exam at school this week and then we can prepare ourselves for the final week before the flower blooms." Mitch had stood up and paced around the table while he spoke. Now he found his chair and sat down again.

I looked everyone in the eyes, "Well I think that's the best plan we have at the moment." I stood up I reached over to put my hand on Mitch's shoulder and thanked him for giving us jobs to do right now. I looked at everyone, their brows were creased with worry. Ava's cheeks were pale, dark rings showed under her blue eyes, Lisa was slouched over the table, worry lines etched around her mouth, Enid was mad, I saw her sorrow at losing Ian, war with her feelings of family and loyalty. Freedom was quietly contemplating his role in the fight. Should he choose family over friends. Mitch gathered Lisa in his arms and whispered in her ear.

I asked them one more time, "Are you all sure this is the path you want to be on, its my families chant, and Ava's. We will continue without you if you choose to leave, we can find a way to save my families lineage. I will let you all think on this overnight, we need to rest and figure out what needs to be handled. I will look in on Majestic right now and see how she is doing. I'll see you all in the morning." I pushed my chair in, and it scraped noisily along the polished floors.

I turned and walked out of the kitchen and headed to the living room where I stopped by Majestic's side. Her eyes were still closed, a healing sleep is what she needed right now. Its what we all needed tonight. I headed towards the guest room off the living room and quietly closed the door behind me, I just needed to rest a few minutes calm before I went to sit in the chair beside Majestic. The bed was so big and comfy my butt sunk into it as I sat and removed my socks. The pillow held my head softly as I closed my eyes to rest just for a minute.

CHAPTER SIXTEEN

Enid

The professor stood up, said goodnight, and left the room. My heart ached, like it was being squeezed beyond repair. I sat at the table and listened as my dad made plans for us to stop the chant from continuing for Ava and Professor Craig's family. I was numb. I looked from my mom to my dad, they loved each other, they spoke freely to each other, told each other their secrets, their innermost thoughts, and desires. I thought I had found that person in Ian. I groaned; I could feel as my heart ripped in two. My dad hadn't stopped touching my moms' hand or her elbow or shoulder since we sat down. They almost lost each other tonight; I almost lost them. What would happen if they lost each other, could they each survive alone? Could I? I looked at Ava, my best friend in the whole world, could I live without her or her without me? We had been a part of each others lives since we were born. What would happen when we broke the curse, I knew we were going to be able to, I just needed a way to get there first. I could sense that we would all get there together. Then I wondered if that were true or if it was something Ian and his family had made us feel.

Ian was a god, a gatekeeper, whatever he was, he wasn't human. Well, he might be right now, but he wouldn't die, he would live forever or until he burned out, just like the stars in the sky. He lit the way for a long time and then he would burn out. How was it that he could control the universe but couldn't help us here? No, that wasn't right, he could help us, but he chose not to, he had walked away from us, from me. I remembered telling him to leave, but I don't think I really meant it. I had been scared, unsure about everything he had told me before he had told me the truth. Was this a part of his plan too? I didn't know what to think, feel, or say. My thoughts swirled in my head a mile a minute. I looked around the table and watched as Ava stood up and left with no words, she just left. Like Ian had. My parents stood together as one and started to clean up the table. Freedom sat still, he looked at the chant book lying innocently on the table. His eyes looked up and met mine, he nodded his head like he knew what I was thinking. I supposed if we must work together; we should start now. The sooner we could figure all this out the better off we would all be. I pushed all the swirling thoughts of Ian to the back of my mind. That would have to be something I worked out later.

CHAPTER SEVENTEEN
Majestic

My head felt fuzzy, my mouth was dry, like I had been sucking on a cotton ball. I should stay and sleep for a little bit longer. I had been drifting in and out for an hour or so. It was dark when I tried to open my eyes, my side felt like it was on fire, but I didn't feel the red-hot pain of literal fire. I remembered all the fire balls that had been hurled at us, me, and Ava. I couldn't remember the ride home, where was I? Oh, the kidnapping, I remembered it now. Enid was supposed to meet me with my car, at a house, a castle really, it was so old. The pain in my head exploded, I felt really dizzy I saw bright white when I closed my eyes, Ugg the pain was to much. I just needed to breathe. In, count to three and out slowly. I felt exhausted just by breathing, my mind cleared, and I passed out once again.

"Halo sister," I turned my head toward my twin, he is glorious, he shone light, like it was made of him. His eyes, my eyes, a beautiful grey and purple mixture glittering with silver flakes stared at me. His skin was a golden-brown and glowed with his inside light it, shimmered and made me feel so warm. I felt like I would never be cold again, his warmth drew me closer to him.

"Your beautiful." I murmured before I realised the words were coming from me. "Where are we?"

"I need to tell you something important Majestic, would you come stand with me? Let me tell you a story."

I tried to walk toward him, but it felt like my feet were on an escalator, I glided silently across the floor, I didn't even feel the floor under my feet. It was an unnerving feeling, but I looked up at my beautiful brother and forget all about it and it only took a second, and I was right beside him, I felt drab and colorless beside him. I am a dark shadow, and he was the light.

"I miss you," I told him quietly "everyday I miss you more, can you come back to me? I need you; we need your help; you know what you are doing, and I feel helpless with all these people who look to me for guidance. Did you know that Enid's boyfriend was a god? Or a gate keeper? It's getting weird, do you feel it? The shift in power? The world seems to be on the brink of war, a disaster will come. I thought we could stop it, but I am feeling that less and less now." Silently I looked into my brothers' eyes and listened to his story.

"We are here and have been for centuries, yes, you and I Majestic. We are the portals to the other world; the gate keepers allow us to travel the worlds in peace because we have a treaty made by our elders. As long as we can keep the balance of good and evil, we can travel freely. I thought long ago when I witnessed the chant being spoken by the gypsy Vano that it was a powerful chant, to powerful, it was going to upset the balance, so I intervened. The gate keepers were angry and forbade my travel to this world for many many years. You are fighting for your mortal life right now because of this imbalance, your death could *be because of my interference. I tried to keep you away, but we are bound by an invisible string, the fate that keeps us on this road will not let us go until our part is complete. I messed up and I got hurt. You miss my mortal body, but I will always be a part of you, we are connected, and we will return together to this world one day again. I hope. This group of people need you, Ava, Craig, Enid, Freedom, even Vano and Rose. I am not able to tell you the part you must play but you will do it. The gate keeper Ian, he will not leave them willingly and I fear he must, this world depends on his leaving. I do not know how his heart break will change the outcome, but he must leave Enid to complete her destiny. Fate is tricky and outcomes can be changed but always remember that any action will in fact have a reaction somewhere. You can help them Majestic; they need you. You must wake up now. I will see you soon sister."*

I tried again to open my eyes what did my brother just tell me, I think I missed the last bit of his goodbye, something about blood. I needed blood. I have blood. I couldn't quite remember what Majic had said, like a slippery noodle it fell through my thoughts like water. I noticed everything at once then. The filtered sunlight that streamed through the windows made little dust rainbows in the air. The colors were warm and bright, but not bright like my brother had been. I had never dreamed of such a beautiful color before. Did I just dream that, could it have been real? He said I was a portal to other worlds. That couldn't be right. These people needed me, that much I got right. I must have made a noise or something because there was a face standing over me looking into my eyes. Freedom.

"Good morning, Majestic. Glad you could come back to us." He whispered softly.

"Water." I mumbled through my dry lips.

"I've got some right here." He held my head up as he put a straw to my lips and told me to take a small sip. It felt like liquid gold as it slipped down my parched throat.

"You gave us a bit of a scare Majestic. How are you feeling?"

"Well, my body feels like I have been run over by a truck, or maybe just shot with a fireball." I smiled weakly at him.

"The second part happened, you must feel the first one because we had to put a sleeping spell on you, so your body could heal. I don't want to alarm you Majestic, but you have been asleep for a week."

A week! Oh no. I hoped that I was not to late to help them break the chant.

"Ok Freedom, tell me everything that has happened since I have been under the sleeping spell."

I struggled to sit up and Freedom was there instantly to help me. He put a cushion behind my back and pulled the table closer so I could rest my legs on it. I felt dirty, I needed clean clothes and a shower. My parched throat was watered but I could tell I needed to now brush my teeth. Freedom sat in the winged back chair beside the couch and started to tell me everything, starting from the day I was hit in the side by the fireball.

Enid and Ian had raced Ava and I back to the house. He told me about the meeting at the kitchen table where they all learned that Ian was a gate keeper and that they had to figure out the recipe that Ava's mom, Katherine, had left for Enid and Lisa. It had been tricky, but Mitch had gotten them inside the gardens to get the Corpse flower scent. The rest of the ingredients had been a bit easier to acquire. They had been stumped on the last item though, *Ichor mixed gently*, the blood of the gods. They thought it must have been Ian's blood they needed, he had told them he was a god, or gate keeper. I opened my mouth to tell Freedom this, but he kept speaking. Enid had tried to contact Ian, but he was unreachable. So, for a week they had poured over books in the library. Everyone was tired and cranky and frustrated. Freedom said he had volunteered to look in on me the most because he felt tension ran high when the curse was brought up, and because it came from his family, he felt their anger. He told me that the curse wouldn't even have been uttered if the professor hadn't cheated the gypsy Vano to begin with. They were running out of time; everyone could feel it. I gently placed my hand over his, it was cold, mine was mysteriously warm until I remembered the feeling of never being cold again that my brother gave to me. I smiled and looked at Freedom who had finally finished his recap of the week.

"I can help." I spoke the words softly.

He looked at me and smiled, "I told them that you could do it. What do we need to do? I need this to end."

"Let's meet in the kitchen, I'm a little hungry" I said as my stomach growled.

"I will let everyone know to come in." He pulled out his phone and started to message everyone.

Majestic is awake and hungry, meet us in the kitchen ASAP.

I heard his phone start to make pinging noises as the responses came fast from the group.

"Ok, everyone will soon be here, lets go get you some chicken broth, or pudding, maybe some milk."

A few minutes later I was seated at the kitchen table and Freedom was standing over the stove warming up some chicken noodle soup he had found in the fridge. I would have preferred something more substantial but his eagerness to help me was endearing. So, I didn't say anything but thank you as he put a steaming bowl of fragrant chicken noodle soup in front of me and handed me a spoon. The tea kettle whistled, and he went to make a pot of tea for everyone who was coming in. He looked comfortable here, like he had spent a few hours in this kitchen. As I consumed the soup, we chatted about nothing important preferring to wait till everyone was there. I noticed the ingredients to the chant recipe sitting on the counter, waiting silently for the blood of a god. I wondered if they knew. Had they even considered the possibility?

My side hurt as I laughed at a little story Freedom told me of his brothers. He looked younger, the lines erased from his forehead but, the hands he folds and unfolds in his lap are a reminder that he is nervous. When I finished my soup, he took the spoon and bowl, washed, and dried them and returned them to their spot. I should tell him, but I can't. Not yet, they must choose. No, not they, she, she must choose. I heard the front door open and close and a few moments later Ava is there.

"Hi Majestic, thank you for saving me. I'm sorry you got hurt."

Her big blue eyes roamed over me as I sat quietly, searching for injury I suppose. They really do look like her ancestors' eyes; Edina would have loved her. I stared quietly into her gaze, I saw the light, my brother was here, he will always be with me. Her eyes glowed with silver flakes for just a second before she blinked, and it was gone. If I hadn't been so intent on looking at her, I would have missed it. She walked over to the cupboard and grabbed a teacup and then went and rummaged in the fridge and cupboards, soon she had made a little snack board for the others, and they arrived one by one, each getting a teacup and a bite of the snack that was set out. Soon we're all arranged around the kitchen table. Their eyes all turned to me expectantly. We had gone over the how are you feeling questions, I wondered how much to tell them, no one had told me not to tell them everything I knew. I was here to help them make sure the balance of good and evil stayed true. I knew there were a million little ways their choices could go, but I also knew they would have an ingrained sense of self preservation. I stood up and walked to the sink and looked out at the garden. It was marvelous. How could I help them choose?

"I would like to thank you for saving me, Enid. And Ava I am truly happy that you were unharmed. My brother still watches over you all. He will continue to do so once we have made the decisions we need to. You all have many choices, make sure you weigh the outcome of each one. Our lives are so small in the big universe however the choice you five make will impact more than you know. What you choose and how you make the choice is yours. But remember, you have had a lot of friends come to guide you in this decision. Do you realise how important it is? A gate keeper chose you five for a reason. Don't make hasty choices please. I believe we shouldn't just leave these choices up to fate or chance or whatever. So, I am going to give you every piece of information I have. My brother visited me, and we had long conversations while I was under the sleeping potion. I miss him dearly. He told me things I needed to hear; I am not sure why he kept this from you but here goes. First, you five are not the first group of people the gatekeepers have put together to solve this chant." I paused a little bit to see the wonder and surprise in their eyes. Enid spoke first, I knew it would be her to question this, her voice was tight with anger.

"What do you mean Majestic? Are you saying others have tried and failed to break the chant that the gypsy Vano cast so many years ago? Are we going to fail also? I know you know the answer, after all we are just pawns right? The universe or whatever knew what we would do. I wonder that we should do anything at all." Enid breathed heavily; her anger evident in her tightly clenched fists that were on the tabletop.

"Enid, your choices are still yours to make. The universe is so vast there are so many options, you cannot give up now. The reason the chant had not been broken is in part because the other groups did give up, they lost their way. You five are strong, stronger than we have ever seen before. Listen, you have all the ingredients, have you made the potion?" I looked around the table, they looked at each other and started to shake their heads. "What is it that you're missing?" I asked them.

"It's the Ichor, its blood from a god. We don't have that." Enid looked at me with tears in her eyes, they filled but did not spill over. "We had him, I had him. Ian was with me for two years and I didn't know he would be the key to the recipe. We need his blood to complete the recipe and break the curse on Ava and her family. And now Ian won't return my calls, I have tried everything to get a hold of him, and he won't answer. The reason we are going to lose, and my best friend will die, is because I sent away the last ingredient, we needed to make the recipe."

Should I tell them, I wondered. My heart beat fast in my chest. I could help them but just this once. It would only be a tiny clue.

"Listen to me closely you guys, you can do this. Ian was just a small setback…"

Enid snorted and interrupted me by saying, "Small? A small setback? Do you know of any other gods who would just wait around to give us some Ichor?"

"You don't need him." I encouraged them, "Think, where could

Ichor be located other than in a god?" I watched them all look to each other, my head started to get dizzy, like I was floating in a bubble of water, "Hey, you guys. I feel funny." I mumbled. Then suddenly I am once again asleep, slumped over the kitchen table.

"Majestic!" Enid jumped out of her seat and rushed to my side. In a few seconds Mitch was there and carried my body to the living room, to the couch, again.

I watched all this as I floated out of my body, just watched them. I tried to tell them that I was ok, but no one noticed me.

Then I heard my brother, "Hey, Maj, you're here again, what did you say to them? The gatekeepers must be mad at you to have brought you back so soon."

I turned my head away from the sight below, they all wondered if the paramedics should be called.

"Hi Majic, where am I now, how come I can see what's happening down there and they can't see or hear me? How do you know it's the gatekeepers who brought me here? What's going on Majic? I need to get back to them. Right now. They need my help; they will fall apart without my guidance."

He smiled brightly at me, "I miss you Maj, why don't you stay here with me for awhile?"

"What do you mean Majic? You know we are here to help this group, it's what we are meant to do, you and I, but now it's only me. This is our destiny this time, you need to help me get back to them."

"I'm sorry Maj, I can't help you do that, you have to find your own way back, listen, I hear the bells calling, I need to leave you now."

I watched as he turned away, he stopped and turned his head toward me and I glimpsed the purple like lightening in his silvery eyes, "GO NOW, help them Maj!" and then his eyes changed to flat grey again and he turned toward the bells and stepped away from me.

I needed to do something; I had felt the pain Majic had felt, he had struggled very hard to tell me to go. Something or someone was hurting him. I needed get back to my body. I still had no idea why I was in this holding platform; it was like a fluffy, soundproof bubble. I couldn't send them any messages; I looked at my body just lying there. Enid was holding my hand and nervously chewed on her lip. Mitch had his phone out and wanted to call 911 but Lisa was stalling him. Ava and Freedom were talking in hushed tones with Professor Craig. What could I do? I tried to float down to my body and enter it, but it was like a cement wall surrounded my human form. I stared intently at my head maybe I could flutter my eyelids or something but no, nothing moved. Oh move, maybe I could write a note or spell a word, I floated to the kitchen and tried to tip the cup over with the tea in it. It was hard and took a lot of concentration, but I did it. The liquid spilled onto the table; I heard Ava enter the kitchen to check on the noise. She went to the counter and got a towel to clean up the spill, so I drifted to another teacup and spilled it over too. She looked up, startled, and picked up the tipped teacup. So, I tipped another and another. She called out to the professor and Freedom to come see and they entered the room with questions in their eyes. The last cup still had a little tea, so I tipped that cup too. A startled sound came from the professor and Freedom seemed to look right at me.

He said, "Is that you Majestic? Are you still here?"

Yes! It's me. I yelled but they couldn't hear or see me.

"Hey, you guys should come in the kitchen." Freedom called to the others.

Soon they were all gathered around the table. Ava still held the wet towel in her hands, the teacups were tipped on their sides and the Professor looked at all the walls. He was looking for me I suppose.

"I think Majestic is here still," Freedom explained to the others.

"Yes, she is right there in the living room laying on the couch." said Mitch as he shook his head, "Ava, did you spill all the tea? Are you okay?"

"I'm okay Mitch, Freedom meant he thinks Majestic is here here. Like in the kitchen with us right now, her spirit maybe." Ava looked around the table and then to the professor. "Can you see her professor? Or sense her?"

"I can feel her presence, but I cannot pinpoint her whereabouts." The professor replied.

Oh please, I am right here, floating above you all, just look up. Suddenly I felt a tug, right in my stomach. Like an invisible string had pulled through my belly button. Whoa! Wait a minute, I am not going anywhere, I belong here with these people. They needed to know where to find the Ichor.

CHAPTER EIGHTEEN
Freedom

Well, this was just getting weird, something or someone just made Majestic pass out, she hasn't died yet, and her spirit or whatever was still here to help us out. It was cool that the teacups had tipped over. Oh, they weren't just tipped over, there were words spelled in the wet brown spill. What did it say? I walked around the table and pushed Mitch and Lisa gently out of my way.

"Hey." Lisa exclaimed.

Mitch just held her elbow and moved them both out of my way and watched me circle the table again. Ava went to put the wet rag on another spill, but I stopped her.

"Wait Ava, I think Majestic was trying to spell something in the spilled tea."

I felt everyone look at me now. "Is that a E or an F?" I walked around the table and Ava started to follow me.

"Look Freedom, it is an F, and this looks like an E!" Ava excitedly pointed it out to everyone so they could see what she saw.

Lisa went to a drawer and pulled out a pad of paper and a pencil.

"Ok we have a definite E and an F, what else do you two see?" she asked us.

"Well, I think this letter could be a D." replied Ava.

"I think Majestic was trying to spell my name." I told everyone.

"It could be mine too." Enid said slowly.

We looked more but we saw nothing clearly, I thought the letters could have been wiped away when Ava tried to clean up the spill.

"Just before Majestic fainted, she said she was going to tell us everything she knew about the chant and the cure. Do you think Ian had anything to do with her fainting? What could Enid or I have to break the chant? We were just bystanders in this problem that Avas ancestors have had to deal with. What could Majestic mean by using either of our names?" I was stumped.

I looked around the table at the people who had become like family to me over the last few weeks. We had to solve this; I could envision us all as we laughed around the dinner table for years to come. This was the family I had been searching for my whole life. A family who cared for one another, they laughed and shared their lives. I had come from a large, distanced family. Some members only cared about this chant and how to make it survive to the end of its course. Others wanted nothing to do with this part of the family, we had been torn in two because of this chant. The lies they had had to tell us as children, the stories made to make us look at this family in hatred. I needed to help them. What had Majestic been trying to tell us?

"She had been speaking about the Ichor when she fainted." Enid reminded everyone "It must have to do with Ian, he is the only god, so the only place we could get Ichor." Her eyes watered again as she realised the man, she loved had left her with no help. "Maybe she meant to tell us that this is my fault and that that was why she spelled Enid in the spilled tea."

"No Enid. I think Majestic was trying to tell us that our names have something to do with the Ichor. Let's go over our story. This had nothing to do with you and I in the present, lets think about this logically." I pulled out a chair so Enid could sit down, and the others followed suit.

I went to the counter and grabbed a clean rag and cleaned up the spilled tea. "Ok, so we know why the chant was cast, it was a case of love between Craig and Edina, and survival between Vano and Lily. The way Vano had felt cheated so he became angry maybe hurt and our gypsy feelings always play into our chants, we must feel the emotions strongly for them to work. This chant has lasted almost to the end, so I know the feelings were very strong. I also know the way to counter any chant is with the opposite feeling. So, we have to be positive, and feel vindicated that the chant has run its course. There is love here, I feel it every time I enter the house. Lisa and Mitch, you have provided the love for the environment and each other, Enid, you, and Ava have the strongest friendship, a kind of sisterly love.

Professor Craig you have the strongest love, you have stayed alive throughout the chant to watch over your children. And I am falling in love with this whole group, you all have accepted me, despite my heritage, and I am made to feel loved by you all every time I am around you." The chandelier above the table brightens and I know its Majestic, I am on the right track.

"I have learned from you all that the greatest love is sacrifice, and you would all die for each other. I would die for you as well." I looked up at the chandelier and imagined I saw Majestic floating up there, her grey eyes were alight with purple lightening.

Before anyone could get up from the table, I grabbed the knife that lay on the counter and run it over my wrists, the pain was fast and hard. I clenched my teeth, so I wouldn't groan out loud. I watched as the red soaked my shirt and dripped onto the floor. It's a minute before anyone moved from the table. It was Professor Craig who reached me first.

"Use my blood, it will work." I say to him in a voice I hardly recognized as my own. It was high and wobbly.

He grabbed a clean teacup and placed it under my wrists and the droplets fell into the clean white cup.

Lisa came over with a clean towel and said, "that's enough." Then she wrapped my wrists up.

I was feeling a bit lightheaded, but my heart soared at the love I had saw in the professors' eyes and now saw in Lisa's eyes. I was getting so tired. I looked up at Ava, Enid, and Mitch they have worried eyes and so I smiled at them.

"Your my family now." I uttered the words as I drifted off to sleep. I was sure I heard Majestic's musical voice as I fell.

"Good job Freedom, we will see you soon."

CHAPTER NINETEEN

Enid

Oh no, what had he done. I had finally decided to listen to the creep, and he goes and tries to off himself, thinking that his blood would work in place of Ian's Ichor. There are no other substitutions for a god's blood. It has to be from Ian, and he is not responding to any of my calls, I had even tried to just yell into the universe. Still no answer. I wondered what Majestic had been trying to spell. Was it my name, after all I had a E and D in my name, what if they were connected? My name and Freedom's. What would have connected us in the history of our families. I was a protector and so were all my ancestors. Oh wait, we were made to be protectors. By Majic, the warlock, but Majestic was his twin sister. They were gods! Well not real gods but maybe like a demigod. So maybe it had to be Majestics blood we used. But how did Freedom fit in. He was an ancestor to Vano, did we need his blood line to break the chant as well, he had said something about feelings, emotions. Strong emotions needed to cast and to break any chant. But the emotions needed come from living people and he tried to kill himself, it didn't fit. I wondered some more. Was it all of us? Majestic told us she knew the answer, then she fainted and hadn't woken up, Freedom knew something and then he was gone shortly after. The professor had spoken some words over him, and he was resting peacefully but he still hadn't woken up. The blood had stopped flowing from his wrists so he would be ok. I knew what it was.

I looked up from the kitchen table where I sat. It looked like grey eyes were watching us. I blinked and they disappeared. Weird. It kind of looked like Majestic's beautiful silvery eyes. I knew it was my blood, I could replace or replicate the Ichor closest. I was enchanted to be Ava's protector, by Majic. He had used his blood in the spell to protect Ava's bloodline. His blood ran in my veins, a demigod's blood. Freedom's blood was needed because he had the emotional tie to Vano, and he had told us he loved us all before he had fainted. My blood is needed because I have Demigod blood. Could I give my blood like Freedom has done? I looked at Ava and knew that I could, I would. I would do everything in my power to save her. It was what I was made for. I noticed the other people in the room. My family, my heart swelled with emotion. Would they understand? Of course, they would, my mom the most because her blood was the closest to mine. The professor was sitting beside Majestic and Freedom in the living room. Ava and my mom were reading the recipe, and my dad was cleaning the dishes in the sink. I looked at the floor where Freedom had fallen, the knife was there and still had his blood on it. There were red smears on the floor where the towel used to clean up Freedom's blood had been dragged over the tiles. I got up from the table and quietly gave my mom and Ava a hard hug. They hugged me back just as hard. They would figure this out, I knew I couldn't tell them what I was about to do. When they let go, I walked over to my dad and smiled and helped with the rest of the dishes. The last item was a glass bowl. We had it for years, I think it was a family heirloom. I smiled at him as he emptied the water and rinsed the rag.

"I will check on the professor, then I will be back, and then we can start the recipe when I return." He kissed my mom on the cheek and left the kitchen.

I bent down to pick up the forgotten knife from the floor and rinsed the blood off in the sink.

"Oh Enid, you don't need to do that, I can clean it up." My mother said to me in a gentle voice.

"Its going to be ok." I replied to her. "Its all figured out now, the chant will be stopped, and Ava will live a long and healthy life."

I watched as my mothers' eyes widened in confusion, just before they narrowed in knowledge, and then she started toward me, her arms stretched out as if to catch me.

Ava looked at me and I watched as her eyes widened in fear. I felt the sharp blade as it skimmed my wrist and the burn as my blood spilled over, it was warm. I watched in slow motion as my red blood slithered down my hand and plopped in the old glass bowl. I would save Ava and her line. I gripped the counter so I wouldn't fall before I had spilled some blood in the old bowl. I saw my dad and the professor rush in from the living room just as I started to slip.

I imagined that I heard Majestic say, "Good job Enid, we will see you soon."

I slithered down the kitchen counter and lay on the cool tiled floor and just before blackness descended, I saw two purple, grey eyes floating near the ceiling.

CHAPTER TWENTY

Ava

What had happened! My heart raced as I ran to Enid across the kitchen. Lisa was right behind me and called out to Mitch. He and Professor Craig entered the kitchen and seeing Enid on the floor they rushed to her crumpled body. The knife lay innocently in the sink with only a smidge of red on its blade. The bowl in the sink held a few red droplets that had fallen from Enid's wrist. The professor grabbed a towel from the closet and tried to wrap Enid's wrists. She looked at him and shook her head no. He helped her to stand while she held her arm over the bowl we watch in silence as a few more droplets landed in the bowl, it made a little splashing sound like a bird in a birdbath did. It only took a few seconds, but it felt like everything had moved in slow motion. I took the towel from the professor and wrapped Enid's wrist up. The professor helped Enid to the kitchen chair she had just vacated to help her dad finish the dishes. She looked sleepy, I watched as her eyes looked to the chandelier, she smiled, and nodded her head then looked at all of us before she fainted dead away. The professor repeated the same words over her as he had to Majestic and Freedom. Then we carried her into the living room and laid her down on the love seat. It seemed to be the only space to lay her. It looked like the three of them, Majestic, Freedom and Enid were having a deep peaceful sleep.

Lisa and Mitch look worried, the professor looked sad and a little defeated. Something had happened here, and I couldn't put my finger on it. It was like the three of them had known something important. But what? I excused myself and started upstairs. I needed a minute alone. A minute to go over all the information again. I could feel the end drawing nearer, we were so close to the ending I could feel it like fresh air on the edge of my tongue. I dropped onto my bed and held my head in my hands. A small sound came from my bathroom.

I raised my head and saw a middle-aged man who held something in his hand. He had long black hair, a medallion tied around his neck with a long piece of leather. He looked vaguely familiar, until he looked me in the eye. His were filled with malice, like nothing I had ever seen before.

"Well, there you are Ava. I have been waiting for you a long time." His voice was raspy, he coughed, and it looked like dust came out of his mouth.

"Who are you, what do you want?" I asked him as I stood up from my bed. I looked and saw that I had closed my bedroom door behind me, we were so far away from the kitchen and living room it would take minutes before anyone would help me if I screamed or if they would even hear me scream. I wouldn't be kidnapped again. My eyes darted around my room looking for anything to use against this dark eyed man.

"No need to scream, we will be headed downstairs shortly." He informed before I could finish the thought in my head. "First let me introduce myself, my name is Vano Romany. I knew Craig long before he became a professor. I am the one that cast the chant on your family long before you were born. It is almost complete and once it is, my family will be free. Your bloodline will be finished. I hold the key right here." He said as he held up the vial of my blood that the kidnappers had taken from me.

"Why my blood? Was it you who kidnapped me? Give it back." I stumbled out the questions as I tried to move toward the door.

He moved silently across the rug, like a ballet dancer, his movements were fluid and graceful. That's it, he reminded me of Freedom, who was lying downstairs. Freedom had wanted to help me and my family, he had said he loved us like a family.

"Here love, let me open the door for you." He seemed so content. He knew what he wanted and how he could get it from us. Of course, he had had hundreds of years to think about it.

Silently I moved out the door and stopped.

"What are you going to do with my vial of blood?" I had to ask, I needed to know the answer before I died, and I knew I was going to die, I could feel it.

Everything we had been working towards so hard would be for nothing. The recipe would do nothing. The three people lying in the living room, who had thought we had time to complete the recipe were hurting for nothing. My eyes teared up as I realised to late the sacrifice, they had made to get us here today.

"Your blood is powerful in a spell Ava," He stated, "Its properties of purity when mixed with a demigod is close to being Ichor and I knew your group of friends were the closest to realising that than any others before you."

He paused a little and then continued, "Your line haunts mine, while yours has achieved goodness, mine has been rife with death, hatred and malice. I am an old man; I would like to die in peace. My wife will be waiting for me on the other side."

Before I could ask anymore questions, we reached the bottom of the stairs. Lisa looked up as I entered the living room. It had grown dark in here, the sunlight faded behind the hills, the lamps had been turned on and they cast an eerie glow along the walls. She gasped as she noticed the man behind me and stood up from beside Enid's still form.

The professor who had been looking at Freedom turned his head and stood as well; Mitch looked up and stared hard at Vano.

"How did you get in?" He questioned the man behind me.

"A little medallion and a chant were all I needed." Vano answered him. A small smile played around his cruel mouth, "You have been quite the unpredictable group."

"Vano, its I, Craig. We met once a long time ago. This is between us, please let my granddaughter and her friends loose. We can finish this once and for all, we are both growing tired." His eyes looked piercingly at Vano. I saw him glance quickly at me, but then immediately returned to the man who stood behind me.

"You are right Craig; this is between us. Why is my grandson here with you? Are you holding him with some spell? Do you mean to take another of my line?" Vano sneered at Professor Craig.

I gasped. What did he mean by *another of his line*?

"Ahh the young one hasn't been told about everything then had she Craig?"

I tried to turn around and face Vano, but he stopped me.

"Did you want to finish the story, Craig? Or should I?"

"What haven't you told us professor?" I asked out loud. I could feel that my life depended on his answer. I felt a sharp poke in my back, not a knife but something sharp. I stood still and waited to hear the answer.

Professor Craig looked at us and then his gaze turned to Mitch and Lisa.

He sighed and then said, "Let's all go into the kitchen and sit."

He turned his back on us and headed away, I felt Vano touch my shoulder indicating that I should move. I turned and headed to the kitchen behind the professor, Mitch, and Lisa. Everyone else sat at the table, but Vano stopped me at the doorway, so we were half in the kitchen and half in the living room.

I saw that the ingredients had been placed around the pot on the stove, everything was ready to add to it and start my spell recipe.

They were just missing my blood, which Vano held tightly in his fist. I heard the professor clear his throat and I looked at him; he looked straight at me. His eyes darted between Vano and me. I looked up and saw grey eyes which looked at us from the chandelier, was that Majestic? Her eyes were the exact replica of her brother; Majic's. I had spoken to him in my dreams, he told me that this would happen, how could I have forgotten that? Suddenly I felt dizzy, oh no, this wasn't going to happen to me too! I needed to hear the story the professor was going to tell. My knees got weak, and I groaned aloud, Lisa looked at me and asked Vano what he was doing to me. I opened my mouth to tell her he wasn't doing anything, but nothing came out. I felt my eyes roll into my head and then I slumped down. Vano caught me under my arms. My vial of blood fell to the floor.

I was positive that I heard a musical voice say. "Good job Ava, we will see you soon."

CHAPTER TWENTY-ONE
Professor Craig

My heart leapt as I watched my last family member as she fell into the arms of my enemy. Were we still enemies? It had been a lifetime ago, many lifetimes actually. Was he here to help break the chant or to ensure we failed at stopping it?

I was unsure but right now I needed to get to Ava to make sure she wasn't harmed. As I took a step toward Vano he looked up and snarled at me, "Stay back Craig."

"Vano, you need my help to move Ava." I told him "Let me

help you move her on to the tabletop, she needs to lay down so I can check her and make sure she is ok. I need to see if what happened to her is what happened to the others."

I waited for his response not moving a muscle. A whoosh of relief left me as he quietly said "ok, let's move her together."

Lisa and Mitch moved the tea set, napkin holder, notepad, and the pencil from the table. The chairs were moved apart to make way for Vano and I to easily place Ava gently on the table. I noticed Vano bent down and picked something red up off the floor he put it in his pocket, but I was distracted by the pale color of Avas face and her shallow breathing. I knew in my heart she would not die, not today. I had seen death many times in my long life, and I knew even if we didn't break the curse, that Ava would live to be fifty years old, it was part of the chant. I checked her over gently to make sure she was breathing regularly, there was color to her fingertips and toes. I put a chair cushion under her head and breathed slowly.

I caught Mitch's eye and nodded my head, "She's going to be ok."

I saw Lisa heave a big sigh, poor woman, she must be frantic, both her girls have fallen into this deep sleep.

"Listen Vano, I have apologised many times over the years, I have put that apology out into the universe. What more can I do? Please help me break this chant. I would like my children to grow old, meet their grandchildren live long lives. Please help us." I begged Vano.

He looked into my eyes and nodded his head, "I am an old man now Craig, I would like to break this chant as well. I will help you. It will soon be time for me to return to my love and I will do it as an honorable man."

He closed his eyes and opened them again. He looked at Lisa and Mitch. "I have known you through many lives and always you are the brave and protective ones. You have done well in your roles."

I watched as he reached into his pocket and pulled out the vial of blood that the robbers had tried to steal from Ava.

"You need to tell Ava what you have done Craig, I will trust you to tell her the history of her blood and why you intervened. Now Lisa, I will need your help, your knowledge of the recipe, I do not think we have much time before your family members and mine never wake up."

"I will tell her the truth Vano, just please finish this chant." I say to Vano while he waited for Lisa to come stand by him.

He rounded the table and stood in front of the stove; the ingredients scattered around him on the counter. The bowl containing Enid's blood was still in the sink and Freedom's blood was beside the sink. Vano gently placed Ava's vial beside it and lifted Enid's from the sink. Lisa took the recipe and brought it to the counter and placed it beside the ingredients, she made a move to step back, but Vano grasped her hand. Mitch stood up to stop Vano, but I stopped him from intervening.

"Lisa, while I chant to join the blood, you must prepare the recipe exactly as it is written, one change can mean disaster. Do you understand?" he looked intently at her until she nodded her head yes and replied, "Yes, I understand."

"Ok lets get this done." He walked over to the freezer and grabbed a bag of ice and dumped it into a big bowl and placed the bowl of Enid's blood in it.

At our startled noises he looked up at us, "Do you really know nothing? Ichor is ice cold. Mixing Enid, Freedom and Ava's blood while I do a chant will result in Ichor. How did you not realise the signs for this? I will tell you a story while we prepare this."

He took a deep breath and started his story; his voice was low and deep and perfectly clear.

"A long time ago, a warlock named Majic heard me in my deepest despair, call out a chant that would result in catastrophic results should the end ever come about. He instructed a raven to watch over the children of the generational chant I had performed. Years and years passed by, and no one could break the chant. His interference allowed the cursed family to live and love, and to see their line continue however, the result was that the matriarch died in her fiftieth year by drowning. Never to see her grandchildren. To me this is a tragedy, family is everything to the gypsy. We live to see our children grow and reproduce and enjoy the traditions we have to share. Our stories are handed down for generations. As the years continued, I watched from the sidelines, the family I had cursed. I watched them love and live their lives never knowing that they were going to die, but I did. I went to every funeral. Over time my hatred of the family dimmed, I tried to undo the chant once and it ended badly. I did not dare try again. When Craig noticed me watching I had just lost a family member, I did indeed manage the confrontation badly. Did you know Craig missed a large part of the story when he told his version to you?"

He looked at me then, "Do you want to clear this up now Craig?" he asked me.

I cleared my throat. "I will finish it from here Vano." I replied slowly.

Vano turned back to the stove and softly sang a song while Lisa helped him to prepare the potion. Mitch sat at the table and listened to me as I continued the tale.

"I was saddened by the loss once more of a dear good family member, taken by the curse placed upon us. I too was saddened by the results of my mistake. I thought I had only wanted to save Edina. By cheating the gypsy, I thought I had saved the girl I loved. I had no idea at my young age that I would be hurting an innocent family. When I happened to see Vano that one day, his anger at me erased my grief. I only wanted to hurt him like he had hurt me. So, I became friends with one of his sons. A friendship we hid, I learned all I could and then I became friends with his son and so on. Each time Vano never knew that I was in their lives, when the time came, I introduced one of my grand daughters to him and they of course fell in love, it was a secret love. Forbidden, but I knew of it and encouraged it. A child was conceived, a son. Through the following years I have encouraged the child and the ones after to continue the blood line. Ava's bloodline. She has the blood of the gypsy and of a warlock. Freedom also belongs to this line, but he did not know until recently. Enid is no casual familiar to Ava; she is the descendant of Majic. For her to be a protector her line had to start with someone. Majic made the raven with the help of his blood. He is a doorway to other dimensions and his blood has been passed on for several generations. It has grown stronger over time."

I paused my story as I heard Lisa gasp. I looked up at her and smiled, "Enid is your daughter Lisa, and Mitch's as well. But she is also made of potent almost god like blood or Ichor. Combining her blood with Ava's and Freedom's will be the closest thing to Ichor we can get without actually having Ichor. I wish that I had known about Ian earlier. I would have tried to talk to him ask him for some Ichor and this would all be over by now. Now that's my story. Ava and Freedom are all I have in this world. I will do whatever is necessary for them to survive. In the end all we have is family and Vano and I, however distant, have bonded ours together. Freedom and Ava are distant cousins." I noticed then that Vano had stopped his singing.

I stopped there and noticed the smoke from the stove curl upward and spread over Ava. She lay silently on the table as a gold droplet fell to her heart and the smoke moved toward her mouth; again, a gold drop fell on her lips. She softly spoke one word, *Tyler*. Then the smoke moved on toward the living room, the four of us followed it and saw it stop over Enid and again it dropped a droplet of golden liquid on her heart then moved up toward her mouth and dropped another droplet. The mist did the same to Freedom and slowly we heard the three of them as they started to stir. A groan came from the kitchen, a dry cough came from Enid and Freedom just opened his eyes. The mist hovered over Majestic, a shimmering droplet of gold fell onto her chest she opened her eyes, and she screamed in pain. I looked at Vano and his eyes were wide with shock. I took a step toward her when suddenly we watched as the whole mist dove into her chest. It was chaos, the noise like being on the inside of a hurricane. The living room erupted with light so bright it burned the eyes. I could hear Majestic scream and the sound grated; my heart broke at the sound. And then it was gone, the loud silence rang in my ears.

I blinked my eyes rapidly and took a giant step toward the couch, but my eyes adjusted to the darkness, and I saw that she was gone. The only thing left behind was a long cylindrical pendant on a long gold chain. She's gone. Just evaporated into thin air. I looked up and saw twin sets of eyes looking down at us, they were silvery with beautiful flashes of purple lightening running through them. One set looked to me and winked, we heard soft laughter and then nothing.

Ava had come into the room and looked to me, "Is it finished? Is the chant broken? I don't feel any different. How are we to know if it worked?" Her beautiful blue eyes look at me in confusion. "Do we know a Tyler? He visited me while I was laying on the table. It was the most peaceful feeling."

"Yes, Vano completed the recipe to break the chant. Majestic tried to tell us what to do but I think, Freedom figured it out first, and then Enid. Ava, you didn't have to do anything, your blood had already been drawn. And I am sorry I haven't heard the name Tyler before; I don't know who you have been visited by, but I hope he means you no harm."

I look at each of them and saw the confusion leave their eyes, slowly it was replaced with joy. I watched as Freedom walked to Ava and hugged her, he whispered something to her that made her eyes water, and she clung to him tightly. I was unsure what I heard but it sounded something like,

I have always wanted a brother.

CHAPTER TWENTY TWO

Tyler

Across the globe a young warlock, named Tyler, shook his head in frustration, his long hair waving in the breeze. Nearby, the Rocky mountains shook with avalanche. The heavy snow toppled down the mountain and crushed the cars driving unaware below. Tyler closed his eyes and thought, *Ian, brother, your making a mistake. You might have broken the chant and stopped it from coming to its conclusion, but you forgot about the tear. It was all for nothing if you cant stop the rain. Should I warn them. Ava still isn't out of danger nor is mankind.*

Tyler stopped the avalanche with a flick of his fingers, and he groaned. *Oh Ian, what are you doing? I will have to ban you from this earth.* Tyler wondered again if he should have answered Professor

Craig when he had called for help. He sighed and remembered that it was not his time to help, not yet. I will give you one last chance to stop the rain; but brother, the floods will come.

Vano would be gone, Craig would be gone, Majic and Majestic would be back in their world, who could help you stop the rain? This time the only life you saved was Ava's. How are you going to save the earth? Brother, I beg you, do the right thing.

He watched silently as the days merged into weeks and then months.

EPILOGUE

Vano and Professor Craig formed an unlikely friendship. This time it was forged with trust and forgiveness. They would both meet their end soon, they knew that and enjoyed everyday like it would be their last. It was early spring when Craig said goodbye, he told everyone that his love was waiting for him, he could see her, in a field of heather, the wind blew her long, sun spun hair gently, her cornflower blue eyes were gleaming with love. He was happy to go join her.

Vano left shortly after. He got to spent time with Freedom whenever he could. He was happy that Freedom had another sister to get to know and they enjoyed introducing her to their family. Vano's wife guided him gently home one night while he slept. There had been a grand feast celebrating his life and his departure. The dancing had continued for days.

Mitch and Lisa lived happily knowing their kids were happy. They had embraced Freedom as the brother they knew the girls had always wanted.

Freedom and Ava had spent months learning all about each other. Ava had met many of Freedom's brothers and sisters, although she was only blood related to Freedom, they treated her like a long-lost sister. Ava finally had a family. She still had dreams of the person named Tyler, he was beautiful if such a word could describe him. She felt his presence but still hadn't met him in person. It worried her from time to time, but she was busy connecting to her new family and trying to spend time with Enid as well. They had grown apart the last few months, Enid had a broken heart and Ava knew she needed time to heal.

Enid was happy for Ava and Freedom, but she felt lonely now that Ava had someone else to look after her. After looking after Ava for so long Enid felt she was no longer needed. Ava was safe, the curse had been broken. Her heart ached everyday though, and she mourned her lost love. She missed Ian. She often wondered if she would ever see him again. She needed to tell him so much, she had been wrong, she shouldn't have sent him away. Every day she walked along the Water of Leith, the beautiful stretch between Balerno and Slateford. The walk was beautiful and quiet. It was easy to forget you were near to a bustling city. It was along this walk that Enid trudged silently over a wooden bridge, when she saw Ian. He stood at the end of the bridge and waited for her. She sprinted across the bridge; her trainers making a slapping sound on the weathered boards. She stopped just before she reached him, her arms outstretched.

"Ian! Is it really you? I've missed you. I'm so sorry I told you to leave, I was hurt and confused. Please stay with me, don't disappear again." She tried to smile through her tears. "I love you; we belong together."

"Enid, I've missed you so much, I'm so sorry I had to leave but I had interfered enough with your lives. I wasn't gone long before I realized I couldn't stay away from you. We do belong together. Come with me." Ian gently folded her in his strong arms. "I will never leave you again. I make this promise to you that we will be together from now till the end of the earth."

"I will go anywhere you are. I need you in my life forever. I have to tell my parents, is that, ok?" She asked him, with hope in her heart. Her arms were still wrapped snuggly around him.

"Of course," he replied "An eternity waits for us. Let's get going."

Arm in arm they walked slowly back down the path she had just come from. It was going to be ok; everything had turned out how it was meant to. Just then Ian felt the splat of water run down the collar of his light jacket. He looked up towards the cloudless sky. Was it beginning to rain? It wasn't just any rain. He knew it was far from finished now. The teardrop was from Vano.

Years before when a young Vano had waited at the gate to the city and he had fast realised that the young redhaired man wasn't going to come with his goat, two chickens and rooster, a tear of anger, rage, despair, and hopelessness had fallen from him. It had only been one tear drop, one tear that could have brought about the destruction of the world. Vano had wiped his face when he saw the young man approach, but it had been to late. He had thought the chant, he had felt the rage. The earth from there had been altered. No matter the broken curse on Ava, the one cast before was still in motion.

Ian took Enid's hand in his and they started to run back to her house. The rain started to fall harder.

What would happen to them now?

Two sets of silvery grey eyes watched the couple as they jogged down the old railway path. They watched as the rain fell in a steady stream drenching them and everything else it fell upon.

Will Ian and Enid be able to save the world with the help of Ava and Freedom? How long would Tyler let his brother struggle among the humans before he intervened?

Find out in the next Star-Crossed novel.

Enid's Choice

Manufactured by Amazon.ca
Bolton, ON